P9-EJY-849

RANGELAND HERCULES

BERKLEY BOOKS, NEW YORK

RANGELAND HERCULES

A Berkley book / published by arrangement with
Transworld Publishers, Ltd.

PRINTING HISTORY
Corgi edition published 1968
Berkley edition / January 1981
Second printing / February 1983

ISBN: 0-425-05965-0

A BERKLEY BOOK ® TM 757,375
Berkley Books are published by Berkley Publishing Corporation,
200 Madison Avenue, New York, New York 10016.
The name "BERKLEY" and the stylized "B" with design
are trademarks belonging to Berkley Publishing Corporation.
PRINTED IN THE UNITED STATES OF AMERICA

For Brian Babani, even though he never
published my Rockabye County stories.

CHAPTER ONE

The Danger of Being an Innocent Bystander

THE wagon lumbered slowly along Hood Street in Austin, capital city of the State of Texas, carrying a pyramid of three huge wine barrels to some saloon or other destination. On its box sat a bulky, bearded driver looking half asleep in the warmth of the late-afternoon sun. Plodding leisurely ahead, the two powerful draft horses appeared to be fully aware of their delivery point, for the driver only rarely found the need to guide them.

Being something in the nature of a business and entertainment section of the city, Hood Street's sidewalks attracted a mixed collection of people. Cowhands fresh off the range rubbed shoulders with town dwellers and ogled the passing women in admiration. Blue-clad soldiers, not quite so hated since the end of reconstruction as practiced by Davis' corrupt and inefficient government, mingled unopposed with supporters of the late Confederate States. A few buffalo hunters strolled along, their grease- and blood-smeared buckskins giving off an unmistakable odor to anybody unfortunate enough to pass close to them. Hanging on the arm of her man, a pretty, garishly dressed lobby-lizzy paraded her wares to anybody who might be in search of female company; and ignored the obvious disapproval of such "good" women who drew aside to let her go by.

Although young, the lobby-lizzy had been selling

her body for long enough to know the genuine customer from the merely curious. Studying the male members of the crowd as the wagon approached, she noted a couple of potential clients and a man she felt she might be only too pleased to offer her services to free of charge.

The man who so attracted the young prostitute's attention would catch the eye in any crowd. Six-foot three in height, his head topped most of the crowd around him. On his head rode a costly white J. B. Stetson hat with a silver concha-decorated band, molded into the shape which marked a Texan to knowing eyes. Clearly he had been making use of a nearby barber shop's facilities, for his curly, golden blond hair showed signs of recent attention. So did his tanned, almost classically handsome face, its cheeks as smooth as only a very good barber could shave them. It was a strong face, with intelligence and humor in its lines. His tan shirt looked freshly pressed and had clearly been made, like his Levi's pants, to fit his frame. That great spread of shoulders, lean waist and long, powerful pair of legs could not be clothed so well from the shelves of a general store. Around his waist hung a fine-quality gunbelt. Matched, ivory-handled 1860 Army Colts, with the Best Citizen's Finish to their metal work, rode in the contoured holsters just right to permit ease and speed of withdrawal.

Everything about the blond giant hinted at wealth. Yet anybody who took him for a dressed-up dude stood a better than fair chance of being rapidly and painfully corrected. He walked with a long, easy stride, light on his feet despite his size, and those matched Colts flared their butts out just right for a reaching hand to grip them with the minimum of movement.

Not that anybody but a stranger to Austin would have made such a foolish mistake as to play Mark Counter for a dude. He had been in the state capital long enough to establish his identity among the citizens. Any member of the great OD Connected ranch ranked high in the matter of salty toughness, and Mark Counter belonged to the elite of the crew, its almost legendary floating outfit.

Born the third son of a wealthy Texas rancher, Mark became rich in his own right when a maiden aunt died and left him all her considerable fortune. He could, if he so desired, have bought his own spread, and he possessed the ability to make it pay. However, he preferred to remain at the OD Connected, siding the man who saved his life in Mexico shortly after the War.* As Dusty Fog's right bower, Mark stood high in the ranch's hierarchy. Many who knew them both claimed that Mark's knowledge of the cattle industry exceeded that of Dusty Fog, despite the other being segundo of the ranch. A dandy dresser, Mark's taste in clothing dictated what the well-dressed Texas cowhand wore; just as during the War he had set the trend in uniforms among the bloods of the Confederate States Army.

Since the meeting at the Appomattox Courthouse brought, if not peace, a cessation of military hostilities, Mark built up a reputation approaching legendary dimensions as a cowhand second to none. Men spoke of his giant strength, told awe-filled tales of his ability in a roughhouse brawl. Yet, skilled as he was, few spoke of him as a gunfighter. In other fields he stood almost alone; there were very few who could equal his muscular prowess. When using his matched Colts he was in the shadow of the fastest, most accurate of all, the Rio Hondo gun-wizard Dusty Fog. Yet the select few in a position to know stated he came a close second in speed and accuracy to his friend.

Normally Mark rode accompanied by Dusty Fog

* Told in *The Ysabel Kid*.

and the Ysabel Kid, a combination hard to beat in the fighting line; and also a factor that prevented his full expertise from showing. Circumstances caused a temporary separation of the floating outfit's leading lights. After helping to bring off a successful peace treaty with the majority of the warlike Comanche nation, * the Ysabel Kid stayed at Fort Sherrard to attend to final details and see his grandfather's *Pehnane* band housed on their reservation. On their return to the OD Connected, Mark hoped to accompany Dusty to the wedding of an old army companion. Receiving a message that his uncle, Tune Counter, needed help against a family of vengeance-seeking outlaws, Mark put off all thoughts of weddings, rode fast to Tennyson and became involved in the affairs of Town Marshal Counter, Calamity Jane and the woman know as Madam Bulldog.†

With the affair brought to a satisfactory conclusion, Mark began his return journey to the OD Connected at a more leisurely pace. His way lay through Austin, and no prominent Texas gentleman could pass his state's capital without paying its sights a courtesy call. Although he found a telegraph message from his employer waiting at the Houston Hotel, he was not surprised; Ole Devil Hardin knew the blond giant's tastes well enough to assume Mark would put up at the city's best hotel. The message told him to stay in Austin for a few days in case Dusty Fog should need further help in untangling the threat to the newly wedded couple's life in their new home.‡

Never one to object to orders, Mark settled down at the hotel and then went out to see what Austin might have to offer a gentleman of taste and discern-

* Told in *Sidewinder*.
† Told in *The Wildcats*.
‡ Told in *McGraw's Inheritance*.

ment. As he strolled along Hood Street, he wondered how his two companions in many a wild celebration handled their chores.

Despite being the state's capital, Austin retained much of the traditional Texas cattle town. The site of the city had been selected in 1836 by a commission appointed from the Republic of Texas' ministers to find the most attractive area in their territory on which to erect the seat of government. After some deliberation they decided on the bluffs over the Colorado River below Lake Travis. The governor's mansion, perched on a hill overlooking the city, the home built for France's minister to the republic and the homes of various civic dignitaries were as fine examples of Southern colonial architecture as could be found anywhere in the country. To the east of those imposing structures rose the home of lesser citizens, their business premises and places of entertainment. Of the latter, Hood Street ranked as the site of many of the better-class saloons, a dance-hall, a theatre, on whose boards trod some of the great names of the day, and gambling houses. No fine colonial dwellings here, only the false fronts and wooden walls to be seen in any other town above the adobe belt.

Suddenly the doors of a saloon across the street from Mark burst open and a scared-looking townsman appeared. Hotly pursued by a screeching saloon girl, the man bounded from the sidewalk on to the street. Realizing that she could not hope to catch him, the girl halted and raised her right hand, which gripped a Remington Double Derringer.

"You lousy, no-good piker!" she squealed. "I'll teach you to go making eyes at that damned Sally-Mae!"

With that she jerked the trigger and cut loose a shot. Even in the hand of a skilled man the stubby Derringer lacked accuracy. Used by a woman who did not spend time at target practice, and who was also wild with indignation and excitement, it became less so. Missing its intended mark by some feet, the .41 bullet punched a neat hole through the ear of the nearside horse of the wine wagon and brought a scream from the injured horse. It reared, forelegs in the air, and swung to crash into its partner. Equally startled by the unexpected assault, the offside horse slammed into its breast harness with some force and swung away from its hurt teammate. Taken by surprise as the wagon swung violently, the driver pitched off his seat and ploughed a furrow in the dirt of the trail.

Dragged forward by the plunging horses, the wagon's wheels scraped on the edge of the sidewalk. Rain running from the edge of the sidewalk porch had eaten away at the edge of the trail and formed a hollow under the planks at the foot path. Usually wagons missed the weakened area, but as this one scraped along its wheels crushed through the crumbling earth and sank down. Doing so brought the wagon to an abrupt halt and caused it to tilt over. Although secured by ropes, the pyramid of big wine barrels began to move dangerously. Nor was their security helped by the rearing and lunging of the two horses; the knots of the holding ropes started to slip. The upper barrel immediately began to sink, forcing the other two apart.

When the wagon raked into the sidewalk the man saw its danger. Thrusting the girl from his arm, he sent her staggering into the wall of the nearest building and bounded along until clear of any possible chance of being caught by the slipping barrels. Shock twisted at the lobby-lizzie's pretty face as she stared at the enormous barrels. Not an intelligent girl, she could still guess what would happen when the ropes parted. She wanted to run, but her legs seemed to refuse the frantic dictates of her mind. Horrified, she watched the ropes moving inexorably toward the point where the knots must cease to function. When that happened all three barrels, weighing well over two hundred pounds each, would come down upon her.

Mark read the situation even more rapidly and took steps to avert it. Leaping forward, he ran by the horses. Long before they could be brought under control, the knots would part. Nor did he think there was time to lift and carry the girl to safety. Even as he reached that conclusion the first rope flew free, fortunately at the center of the barrels, although that would merely speed the disintegration of the other knots.

Halting with his back to the girl, Mark placed both hands against the center of the bottom barrel. The forward knot came free, its end whipping into the air, and a moment later the last fastening parted. Instantly Mark felt the barrel begin to move. Gritting his teeth, he braced himself against the weight. His shirt swelled and writhed as the muscles of his shoulders took the strain. Though ample, the cloth of his shirt sleeves drew tight under the expansion of his deltoid and biceps muscles. The boots he wore had been made by the El Paso leather worker Joe Gaylin, designed so that their high heels would spike into the earth and hold firm against the pull of a wild horse or longhorn bull when roping on the ground. Often Gaylin claimed that nothing short of a miracle could rip the heels from any boots he made and, not for the first time, Mark concluded the old timer spoke nothing but the truth. While they had not been made to grip on wood, the heels caught and held at a time when to slip would have been fatal.

Attracted by the sound of the shot, people gathered quickly about the wagon. Seeing what confusion her shot had caused, the saloon girl put aside thoughts of extracting revenge on the fleeing man and disappeared hurriedly into her place of employment. Although a good-sized crowd formed, at first nobody made a move to help Mark. Amazement

at the feat of strength they were witnessing held men
and women alike immobile. At first it seemed impossible for even so large and powerful a man as
Mark to hold the barrels, but he did so, despite the
jerks caused by the two horses tugging at their harness.

Then help came. Thrusting himself through the
crowd, a tall, middle-aged man in range clothes took
in the scene and acted fast. From his hat down to the
high-heeled boots on his feet his clothes spelled Texas
cowhand, lean as a steer raised in the greasewood
country. His tanned, moustached face bore an expression of authority. Certainly he gave orders like a
man long used to doing so.

"Grab those hosses' heads and hold 'em still, one
of you!" he barked. "And let's have some help down
there."

Given the stout guidance and leadership of the
cowhand, a man leaped to lay hold of the horses'
reins. Swiftly he brought the animals under control,
even calming down the injured one. However, the
cowhand found difficulty in persuading other members of the crowd to follow him. If the barrels rolled
from the wagon's bed, anyone who got in their way
stood a better than fair chance of being spread like a
flapjack over the sidewalk.

Only the barrels did not roll off. Exerting all of his
giant strength, Mark not only held them but started
them back into their original place. Slowly, almost
imperceptibly, the top barrel started to inch its way
upward under the pressure of Mark's push. Sweat
poured from a face that bore mute signs of the
tremendous effort he made.

"Come on, blast you!" yelled the lean cowhand,
walking swiftly along the boards until he reached
Mark. "Hold her steady, boy, I'm coming by."

Carefully avoiding touching Mark, the cowhand
stepped by him and ordered a couple of men
following him to watch how they moved. Clearly a

man of decisions and action, the cowhand snapped rapid orders which received immediate obedience. Two men on each side of Mark got their hands to the barrel and, adding their strength to his, forced the bottom barrel back to its original place while the cowhand grabbed hold of the first rope.

"Just keep her steady, boys," he said and started to fasten it to the side of the wagon. "Hold it while I get the other end."

Passing behind the men, the cowhand knotted the second rope into place. He then crept under the barrel holders and secured the central fastening. Checking on the security of the knots, he backed out and nodded in satisfaction.

"Ease off slow and easy until we see if they'll ride," he suggested.

Carefully the men relaxed their hold on the barrels, ready to stop them should there be any sign of movement. None came and they stepped clear, grinning in the pleasure of achievement. Pushing herself from the wall, the lobby-lizzie ran to Mark's side and steadied him as he staggered slightly. For a moment he struggled to catch his breath, then rubbed a hand across his brow.

"You saved me!" the girl gasped, clutching at his arm. "I thought I was a goner for sure."

"Now that'd be a real waste," Mark replied, having recovered enough to take an interest in the object of his rescue. "I'm———"

At that moment his eyes located a member of the crowd who made him forget whatever he had meant to say. While the lobby-lizzie was real pretty, she could not compare with the girl who caught and held Mark's attention. Topped by a stylish little hat, flaming red hair framed a truly beautiful, almost regal face. Nor did the figure below detract from the beauty of the features. The elegant dark dress of the latest Eastern cut emphasised the rich curves of a magnificently proportioned female body. Expensive jewelery, in perfect taste, flickered on the girl; just enough of it to add to her charms. As she stood at the side of a man Mark knew to be the president of the Land & Trust Bank, the beautiful young woman's face lost its expression of concern and took on one of blank lack of recognition.

"She'll hold if they pull her out easy, Mark," said the cowhand whose timely arrival had jolted the crowd into assisting the blond giant.

"Huh?" Mark grunted, jerking his eyes from the gorgeous redhead to the speaker. "Hey there, Tule, long time no see."

"That's for sure," grinned the cowhand. "You could've got hurt just now."

"Somebody had to do something."

"And you was fool enough to do it. All you Counters're the same."

Having been with Mark's father ever since Big Ranse Counter had come into Texas and helped to build the great R over C ranch, Tule Bragg could speak with some authority on that subject. From his birth until riding off to join Bushrod Sheldon's Confederate cavalry during the Civil War, Mark had known and respected Bragg as second only to his father. From Bragg came much of Mark's knowledge of cattle work, the foreman being an acknowledged master in that field.

Although the lobby-lizzie showed willingness to stay by her rescuer she received no inducement to do so. Knowing better than to force her attentions too closely, she joined her man and proceeded to tell him at length what she thought of his desertion. He took it, deciding that a man who risked an unpleasant death to save a girl would be just as likely to take her side if he saw her being abused. Besides, time was passing and Austin offered too many alternative sources in the girl's trade for them to waste time. Taking her arm, he steered her off along the sidewalk and through the crowd. In passing, the lobby-lizzie darted a curious glance at the beautiful redhead and wondered if it had been she who had attracted the blond giant's attention.

Having recovered from his involuntary dismount, the wagon's driver swung back onto the box. Carefully he guided the horses forward and eased the wagon away from the sidewalk. When he was sure that there was no danger of a further tipping, he continued on his way.

"What's brought you up this ways, Tule?" Mark asked after they had seen the wagon safely on its way.

"We're running a herd of Mexican cattle up to Newton," Bragg replied. "Your pappy bought 'em below the border and reckoned to sell off the steers to cover it."

"Pappy coming in?" Mark inquired hopefully.

"Nope. He sent me to handle some business and figures to let Sailor Sam fill up the chuck wagon here."

"When'll Sam be here?"

"Late tomorrow or the next day, depending on how the herd moves."

A grin came to Mark's face at the prospect of meeting his father's cook again. At some time in his youth Sailor Sam had followed the sea as a career and had also picked up a sound, thorough knowledge of fistfighting. It had been the cook who'd taught Mark most of what he knew about defending himself with his barehands. Nor did Sailor Sam belong to the stand-up-and-slug school of pugilist thought. Instead he'd taught Mark to block punches, dodge, weave and hit accurately in a way which disconcerted opponents trained in the old slugging school. So Mark looked forward to seeing his old teacher. With any amount of luck, a city the size of Austin ought to hold somebody desiring to prove he, or they, could fight. If that was the case, Mark and Sailor would be only too willing to oblige and the blond giant could show how well he'd learned his lessons.

"I don't want Sailor getting all stove up in no fist-fight," warned Bragg, following the blond giant's train of thought like a bluetrick hound laying after a raccoon.

"Yah!" Mark replied. "You're beginning to sound like that schoolmarm you was sparking back home."

"Blast it, boy!" bristled Bragg. "I never sparked no schoolmarm. You danged Counters figure everybody's like you, always a-chasing some poor unfortunate gal. Tell you, I figured you'd take off that pretty bachelor's wife you done rescued and give her a fate they reckon's worse'n death."

"That's a real offensive remark to make to the boss's son," Mark grinned.

"Your pappy'd fire me for it, only he figures that everybody'd say he done it 'cause he can't lick me at poker," Bragg answered calmly. "To show you that I didn't mean it, I'll let you buy me a meal."

"Damned if I see why I should buy you the meal," Mark said. "But it'll save arguing if I do. Let's go eat."

Saying it, he looked to where the beautiful redhead walked by on the arm of the banker. She did not look the blond giant's way, and he did not offer to speak. Following the direction of Mark's gaze, Bragg grinned.

"What's that jasper got that you haven't?"

"A fancy dude suit, a paunch, a gold watch chain and a bank," Mark replied.

"Don't worry none," Bragg consoled him. "Maybe you'll have the suit, gold watch chain and bank one day. You've already got the paunch."

"That being the case, maybe we'd best not eat," Mark drawled.

"I said you'd got it, not me," Bragg replied. "So you're not getting out of buying me a meal that ways."

CHAPTER TWO

A Question of Ownership

AFTER a hearty, if leisurely, meal at the Bon Ton Eating House, Tule Bragg looked at Mark with a broad grin.

"Now what do we do, boy? This here big city's got to have some mighty evil temptations for us country boys to avoid."

"Let's go take a look for them then," Mark replied, shoving back his chair. "Like Pappy allus says, a man doesn't know which kind of temptations to avoid unless he tries them."

After paying for their meal, Mark led the way out of the building. Night had come and lights glowed invitingly from various places of entertainment. Already the sounds of revelry reached their ears. Pianos, growing tinnier and more discordant the farther east they originated along Hood Street, rattled out a variety of tunes. As the quality of saloon improved, so did the music offered grow in volume and number of available instruments. After studying the bill for the theatre, Mark and Bragg decided that it offered nothing they wished to see. So they continued strolling in the direction of the Bigfoot Saloon, the largest, most expensive place in the area if not the whole town.

"Hey, look up there!" Bragg said, catching Mark's arm and pointing into the sky to where a streak of light flickered through the blackness.

"It's nothing but a shooting star," Mark replied.

"It's nothing but a sign, boy," corrected the foreman. "Why every time I see one my luck's running high and can't be beat."

Which meant, as Mark knew full well, that their night's entertainment and study of temptations would not go far beyond some gambling game. In addition to being a tophand with cattle, Bragg was also an inveterate gambler. Let him once see what he felt to be a sign of any kind and he headed for the nearest game of chance on the run.

Leading the way into the Bigfoot Saloon, Bragg paused and looked around him. Not that he had eyes for the fancy fittings, the display of choice types of drinks behind the long mahogany bar, nor the attractive, gaily dressed girls all hot and eager to join any customer who wished for company. Instead Bragg glanced around the various ways in which the management allowed their clientele to wager money. Ignoring the blackjack and chuk-a-luck layouts, for he knew no man could hope to beat the house's percentage at either, Bragg searched for a poker game and did not find one of the kind he wanted: playing straight, with no wild cards, fancy hands or limit. Failing a chance to match his wits in a top-class poker game, his eyes went to where a sign with a painting of a tiger hung over a big table.

"Let's go buck the tiger for a spell," he suggested. "The signs tell me I'm set to howl tonight."

"The last time they did that you lost a month's pay," Mark reminded him.

"That was 'cause I mixed the signs up," replied Bragg. "I'm older and some slicker now."

Nobody knew who first used the sign of a tiger to advertise that faro was the game played, but the two had become synonymous. Being conservative by nature in their hatred of change, gamblers also demanded that the table's layout remain the same. So, whether thirteen real cards were used, the symbols chalked on rough planks, scratched in dirt or tastefully stained upon green baize cloth, players insisted that spades be used. Laid out in two rows of six cards, from ace to king, with the seven on its own at the left center of the rows, the layout varied only in the nature of its making.

Already eight players sat at the table, but the game had not yet begun. Facing them across the table, the dealer riffled a deck of cards with practiced skill. Before him stood the dealing box, open at the top so that only one card at a time would be available. However, the cards could not be removed from the top during play, but had to be slid through a narrow slit on the side facing the players. A small spring in the bottom of the box held the remaining cards firmly against the top of the frame.

While the dealer sold stacks of chips from the rack placed at his right hand, to his left the casekeeper prepared to play his important part in the game. Looking something like an abacus, the caseboard carried pictures of the thirteen spade cards instead of numbers and four wooden balls rested on each symbol's wire. As the casekeeper pushed all the balls to the left side of the frame, the lookout mounted his high stool, from which he watched the entire action, ensuring that bets were paid off correctly and preventing any chance of cheating.

"I'll take a stack of them fancy yeller chips, friend," Bragg announced.

Mark had already studied the chips and seen the small marker stamped with the numerals 200. That meant the twenty chips in the stack cost two hundred dollars, or ten dollars each.

"Same for you, mister?" asked the dealer, looking at Mark.

"Nope. I'll just watch a spell," the blond giant

replied and guessed it would be some time before Bragg pulled out of the game.

After a thorough riffling of the cards, the dealer offered them to be cut. Everything seemed to be fair enough to Mark, and he doubted if a place like the Bigfoot would resort to cheating. The dealer's box had an open top, a sign of honesty. "Sand Tell" cards, specially treated for cheating at faro, could be used only from a special box with a closed top and small hole left to thrust out the cards. The big stake table in a saloon of the Bigfoot's quality attracted professional gamblers capable of detecting any cheating device and men of sufficient social standing to make things very awkward for a saloonkeeper who crossed them. So Mark figured nothing but luck would separate Tule Bragg from his savings during the game.

Luck alone won at faro, especially during the early stages, which was one of the reasons Mark did not play it. When he gambled he wanted to use some skill and to be able to play the cards himself.

"Lay on your bets, gents," said the dealer after the cut had been made and the cards placed into the box.

"I'm betting the seven to win," Bragg told Mark, placing a chip in the center of the appropriate card on the layout. Then he moved between the two and three, but placed a hexagonal black marker on it. "And coppering the deuce and trey seeing's they both owe me some loser's money."

All the other players set down their bets, following the various methods of indicating whether they wagered on one card or a combination of two, three or four. Carefully the lookout watched every bet, memorizing them so as to act as mediator in case of disputes. For that reason lookout men needed to be intelligent, cool and tough enough to back their decisions against objecting players. One player set down a red chip on the table level with the represented deuce and in front of the dealer to indicate that he bet the winning card each time would be an even number.

"All bets down?" the dealer inquired and received a chorus of agreement. "Here we go then, gents."

With that he slipped the first card out of the box. Known as the "soda," it was dead and could not be used in the play. Placing the soda alongside the rack of chips, he drew out the next exposed card and put it down at the right of the box.

"Deuce loses," he told the players and indicated the seven of hearts at the top of the box. "Seven's a winner."

Which meant that Bragg collected on two of his bets during that "turn" of two cards from the box. Sliding out the winning seven, the dealer placed it on the "soda." Already the casekeeper had run along one of the jack's buttons to touch the opposite side of the frame and show that one of the four had been taken out of play as the "soda." Next he moved the first deuce marker clear across the frame to signify it lost. The winning seven was shown by its button on its wire being halted half an inch from the edge. In a well-conducted game the "case" offered a visible and accurate record of every card played and what its result might be.

Once again the dealer drew out the exposed card and placed it on the loser pile at the right of the box, showing the winner card underneath. While faro interested its players, Mark found being a spectator boring. He knew that Bragg would object to being disturbed, so turned and walked across to the bar. A group of well-dressed men stood there, and Mark recognized one by the name of Shangai Pierce, a prosperous rancher and friend. Letting out a cowhand whoop, Pierce extended a powerful hand to Mark and introduced the blond giant to the rest of the party. Next Pierce demanded to be told how the

treaty council went, something in which every man at
the bar had an interest. So Mark told them what had
happened, making lurid oaths as he mentioned the
attempts by both white and Indian elements to
prevent the affair being brought to a successful conclusion.

"Look who's just come in," Pierce growled,
nodding toward the main entrance. "Know 'em,
Mark?"

Turning, Mark looked the new arrivals over. In
front strode a big, heavily built man. A battered
high hat sat on a mop of shaggy greying hair, the
face under it lined and seamed until it disappeared
into the mat of beard. He wore a wolfskin jacket,
tartan shirt, Levis pants tucked into calf-high
Indian moccasins. Around his waist hung a gunbelt
with a Dragoon Colt butt forward at his right side
and tomahawk in slings on his left. All in all, he
looked a mean, hard customer who would make a
bad enemy.

Behind him came three younger men, all showing a
certain family resemblance. They wore range clothes,
yet Mark did not take them for cowhands. At the
bearded man's right side stood a tall, handsome
jasper. Dandy-dressed, he sported a gunbelt with its
holster fitted to it by a rivet-swivel, the tip of the
Colt's long barrel poked through the bottom and not
by accident. At the dandy's left and behind the big
man was a gangling beanpole in his early thirties, untidy in appearance but wearing a brace of Cooper
Navy revolvers in low hanging holsters. The last of
the quartet had a medium-height, stocky-built frame,
red hair and belted two Freeman Army revolvers butt
forward in low cavalry twist-hand holsters.

While the quartet gave the impression of salty
toughness, they did not particularly worry Mark.
Nor could he see them causing the burly rancher at
his side any great concern. In addition to owning a

big Texas ranch, Shangai Pierce bore a well-deserved name for handling salty toughs no matter how they came.

"Can't say I do," Mark admitted. "Who are they?"

"Big jasper's Churn Wycliffe, runs a trading post and hoss ranch up the top end of Lake Buchanan," explained Pierce. "The flashy dresser's his nephew, Billy Wycliffe, and claims to be fast with that fancy, half-breed holster. T'other two're kin. The bean-pole's Loney Sandel and the last one's Evan Shever."

After looking around the room Churn Wycliffe spoke to his companions. Billy grinned and made some reply, indicating the bar, only to have the big man snarl back at him. Then Wycliffe stamped across the room to where a tall, thin, bearded man in a top hat, frock coat, dirty collarless shirt and patched pants sat nursing a glass of beer at a table. Nodding a greeting, Wycliffe sat with the man and signaled to a waiter. His companions stood undecided for a moment and then trooped across to the high-stake faro table. Billy took the last chair and the other two jostled a space for themselves, Evan Shever sitting on the edge of the table and grinning at the dealer in a challenging manner. However, the trio knew better than make too much of a nuisance, for the Bigfoot Saloon's bouncers could be mighty per-suasive in such cases.

"Trade must be good," Mark remarked, turning back to the bar.

"Likely," Pierce replied. "Only I wouldn't want to guess at where they get the stuff they sell—or how."

"It's not off Jake Jacobs there, that's for sure," another rancher in the group stated. "He's a pedlar but he don't often have anything of value to sell."

"Are they wanted?" asked the youngest man present, a touch eagerly.

"Nope," admitted Pierce. "More 'cause nothing's been proved on them than for any other reason." Clearly, thinking of the Wycliffe clan's possible criminal tendencies brought something more to the rancher's mind for he went on, "Say, the Bad Bunch've pulled another one."

"What's it this time?" asked a prominent businessman.

"The Wells Fargo office in Fort Worth while the governor was handing out prizes at the county fair there. Knifed the agent and nobody saw a thing."

"I wonder who they are?" breathed the youngest man; he worked for the local newspaper and longed to be in on a big story that would bring him national acclaim, or at least the chance of being hired by one of the Eastern daily papers.

"Dick Dublin and the Kimble County boys," guessed one of the crowd.

"Not them!" snorted the second rancher. "It's the Marlows."

"When Alf Marlow or any of his kin get brains, you'll maybe convince me they're the Bad Bunch," snorted a man from the Fort Ewall country, full of civic pride and extending it to cover the leading light of his area's criminal element. "It's Jim Moon and his bunch."

A comment which aroused considerable derision among the other members of the crowd, all of whom appeared to favor some different outlaw as leader of the mysterious gang called, for want of more information, the Bad Bunch. In fact, the discussion began to grow heated, and Mark felt that he ought to put a damper on it in the interests of peace and quiet.

"I reckon it's time we had another drink and talked about women," he declared, as an otherwise peaceable pillar of East Texas society demanded instant recognition of Cullen Baker as brains, leader and organizer of the Bad Bunch. "Which same it'd be one helluva note if some of you gents were thrown in the pokey for brawling over which owlhoot's the best.''

A point that the others readily accepted, especially a well-known lawyer from South Texas who had been vehemently insisting that Bill Brooken—later sentenced to *one hundred and twenty-seven* years in prison—alone possessed sufficient savvy to run the elusive gang.

At that time Mark had no interest in the identity of the Bad Bunch. Soon circumstances would bring him into contact with them, and they proved to be more than the cream of the floating outfit could handle.*

Wishing to change the subject, he told of his last meeting with Calamity Jane and gave details of her defeat at the hands of Madam Bulldog, while omitting to mention the surprising fact which emerged concerning the woman who out-cursed, -drank, -fought and -shot Calamity.

"Last I heard she was up Utah way, driving a stage,'' Pierce remarked. "Calamity, I mean. Helped U.S. Marshal Cole to bring in a gang of owlhoots.''

"Cole?'' repeated the lawyer from South Texas. "I knew a Cole used to ride in Captain Jack Cureton's Rangers in the War. Is that the same jasper?''

"Sure is. He's my cousin,'' Mark agreed and wondered how Solly Cole had got on with the volatile Miss Martha Jane Canary.†

The subject changed to less provoking subjects than the identity of the Bad Bunch. After some of the Calamity Jane stories had been passed around, the men turned once more to Texas' major industry and talking point, cattle. After a short time Mark remembered Tule Bragg and decided to take the foreman a drink. So he ordered four fingers of Old Scalp Lifter

* Told in *The Bad Bunch*.
† Told in *Calamity Spells Trouble*.

and carried the glass across the room.

"Five's the loser," announced the dealer. "Pay the coppered bet on it."

"That's mine," Billy Wycliffe stated.

"The red chip may be," Bragg put in quietly. "But that yellow with the copper on it's mine."

Silence dropped on the table and the other players began to draw away from the speakers. Under cover of the movement, Sandel eased around to halt on the opposite side of Bragg to his cousins. Mark found no difficulty in reaching the table due to a sudden and hurried withdrawal of standing players and kibitzers. In Texas a question of ownership around a card table could result in some fast, deadly and convincing arguments being used.

Slowly Billy began to swing on his chair seat in Bragg's direction. At the same time his hand moved toward the Colt's butt. Using a swivel-mounted holster, he did not need to draw the gun but could turn it still in the leather and fire through the bottom. Mark did not know whether Bragg had noticed how young Wycliffe wore the Colt and felt disinclined to wait and see. Not wishing to spill the drink in his left hand, the blond giant held it out to the side. Bending, he gripped the right rear leg of Wycliffe's chair in his free hand and jerked it from under the dandy.

Letting out a yell of surprise, which turned into a yelp of pain, Billy lit down rump-first on the floor. In their own area, the Wycliffe clan packed considerable weight and authority. Few men around San Saba would cross them, and so they expected the same to apply wherever they found themselves. Unfortunately for their peace of mind, Mark Counter cared little for reputations and showed respect only to those who warranted it.

From the corner of his eye, Mark saw Shever drop from the table and reach for his gun. Bringing up the chair in a back-hand swing, Mark crashed it straight into the stocky redhead's face. Bright lights seemed to burst before Shever's eyes and he reeled backward, tripped, then sat down hard. After which he flopped on to his back, losing all interest in the proceedings.

Like Shever, Sandel did not expect such a prompt, devastating disrespect to be shown for the Wycliffe clan. However, he considered it necessary to assert the family superiority, in the interests of maintaining their reputation of having never been curried below the knees. So he snaked a hand toward the off-side Cooper's butt. The move was fast, although not exceptionally so, and might have been capably performed had he been permitted to finish it.

When settling down to play, Bragg had removed his hat and hung its storm-strap on the back of the chair. He invariably kept his hair cropped short, which turned his head into a mighty effective weapon as Sandel discovered. Leaving his seat with surprising speed, Bragg butted the gangling Sandel in the belly. There was not even a growth of hair to cushion the impact, so Sandel felt like he had been struck in the stomach by either a cannonball or a charging bighorn ram. Pitching backward, his hands folded on the injured area and he doubled over to collapse in a retching, twitching pile in the sawdust.

Across the room Churn Wycliffe threw over his chair, rose and started to reach for his Colt. Figuring that the man ought to be taking a hand at about that time, Mark had already swung to face him. The chair dropped as Mark's right hand flashed down. Fingers curled around the smooth ivory handle of the right side Colt and slid it from leather. As it came out, Mark's thumb eased back the hammer; but his forefinger remained straight along the triggerguard until the eight-inch barrel slanted away from him. In slightly over three-quarters of a second, a cocked, lined Colt pointed in Churn Wycliffe's direction with a finger around its trigger all set to turn lead loose.

That was the kind of smooth, practiced speed and ability which set the top gun apart from a man who was merely fast. Churn Wycliffe could read the signs and recognize Mark's true potential as easily as a schoolteacher going through a child's first addition papers. Such speed only rarely came without an equal skill at placing the bullets in any desired area. Nothing about Mark led Wycliffe to believe he faced an inaccurate exception. So the burly man spread his hands away from his sides in clear proof of his pacific intentions.

"Take it easy, friend," he said in a voice deep as the growl of a Texas grizzly chewing cow meat. "And you-all, Billy, you stop that right now."

Spluttering curses, Billy had swung around still seated on the floor and reached toward his Colt. At his uncle's bawled-out command, he removed his hand. Or it could be that he heard the cocking click of Bragg's Dance Bros. Army revolver as the foreman threw down on him.

"The boy shows some sense, mister," Bragg drawled as Wycliffe walked up. "Only not at a card table."

"Mind telling me what's up?" Wycliffe inquired with surprising mildness, or so it would seem to anybody who knew him.

"I coppered a bet on the five, he didn't and the card came out a loser," Bragg explained. "So he tried to claim my bet."

"That true, boy?" demanded Wycliffe as Billy climbed sullenly erect.

"It's my———" Billy began.

"Don't lie to me!" bawled Wycliffe. "You didn't have enough to buy yellow chips at this table. How about it, lookout?"

"That was the gent there's bet, the coppered yellow," the man in the lookout chair replied, indicating Bragg.

CHAPTER THREE

A Visitor for Mr. Counter

FOR a moment Billy Wycliffe stood glaring at the lookout as if he could not believe his ears. Nobody up around San Saba would have dared to go against the wishes of a Wycliffe. What Billy failed to recognize, but his uncle saw all too clearly, was that they had passed out of their sphere of influence. While they could claim to be real big fish in their own small pond, the same did not apply in Austin. Not only did the blond giant dress well and handle a gun like a master, but he had been in some mighty important company. Any man on such amiable terms with Shangai Pierce, to say nothing of the other dignitaries at the bar, could not be shoved around like some small town cow-nurse.

That fact alone weighed heavily, but Wycliffe had another point to take into consideration. Jake Jacobs might not have a high-class range of wares to peddle, but he supplied top-grade information on a number of subjects if the price be right. What the pedlar passed on to Wycliffe made the burly man decline to become involved in trouble; especially against so obviously capable a man as the blond giant. Jacobs' information called for the services of all the men Wycliffe could lay hands on. He stood a good chance of losing, permanently or temporarily, at least a portion of his help should they push the matter further.

"You hear the man, boy?" he growled at Billy. "Now just tell the gents that you're sorry for the mistake."

"Like———" Billy started to say.

A big hand clamped hold of his shirt front, bunching it up and shaking him like a terrier with a rat. Looking at his uncle's face, Billy felt scared.

"You do it, boy!" ordered Wycliffe. "You hear me now!"

Set back on his feet, Billy glared his hatred at Mark and Bragg. For all that, he spat out. "All right, so I made a mistake."

"Now get the hell out of here!" Wycliffe ordered. "And take Cousin Evan with you."

Muttering under his breath, Billy helped the moaning Shever up. With his cousin's arm around his neck, feet dragging along, Wycliffe started for the door. Wycliffe stepped to Sandel's side and hoisted him on to his feet. Snarling a curse, he slapped the beanpole's hands away from the Coopers and shoved him after his two cousins.

"Damned fool kids these days," Wycliffe said, watching the trio leave. "I don't know what the hell they're coming to. No hard feelings, gents?"

"There's none on my part," Bragg assured him.

"Or mine," Wycliffe declared.

"You'd maybe best watch them, mister," Mark put in. "They could get hurt if they come fussing around me again."

"I'll see they don't," Wycliffe promised and nodded to the glass Mark held. "You've got a mighty steady hand, friend, never spilled a drop."

Which was the truth. All through the hectic few seconds of his intervention, Mark neither dropped nor spilled any of Bragg's drink. Twirling away his Colt, he corrected the lapse by tossing the contents of the glass down his own throat.

"I did now," he said. "You'll watch them three, mister?"

"We're just now pulling out and won't be back," Wycliffe replied. "No hard feelings on either side, I hope, gents."

With that he turned and walked out of the room. Some of the crowd looked disappointed that the affair ended so tamely. Others showed their relief at not being too close to a gun battle where stray bullets might start flying. Naturally such an event could not pass without discussion and comment.

"That's the first time I've seen the Wycliffes back off," said one of the players at the chuck-a-luck table. "They don't go that easy most times."

"Most times they're not up against one of Ole Devil's floating outfit," the man handling the dice cage replied.

"Is he Dusty Fog?" inquired another player.

"Nope. Mark Counter."

"Man. If Dusty Fog's faster than him, that's real rapid."

"You expecting a war, Shangai?" asked Mark, returning to the bar for a replacement drink.

With a grin, Pierce slid his Colt back into leather. "It's not every day you see Churn Wycliffe sing low that ways. Not that I blame him, mind."

Which, coming from a man who made more than one allegedly tough Kansas trail town marshal hunt for his hole, was quite a tribute to Mark's ability and toughness. The general feeling in the place seemed to be that Mark acted in the best possible manner and showed considerable tolerance in not taking more severe measures against the trio. So the house manager raised no objections to the blond giant's continued presence; although he told the bouncers to make sure that none of the departed Wycliffes returned. While a gunfight brought publicity and an increase in trade, it could also come a mite expensive to the fittings and furnishings.

Mark had intended to leave after buying Bragg the drink, but changed his mind. Not a man to back away from any trouble forced on him, he did not go out of his way looking for it. If Churn Wycliffe wanted to take his nephews out of town and so avoid further friction, Mark had no desire to prevent him from doing it. To walk outside while they gathered their horses could be interpreted as an open challenge.

"You figure they'll leave, Shangai?" he asked.

"If Churn says for them to, they will," the rancher stated. "Those three and all the clan're real scared of him. What're you fixing to do now?"

"Have another drink and go," Mark replied. "Way Tule's stacking up the chips, it'll be a fair piece afore he's ready to leave. So I'll be on my way."

"There wouldn't be a gal around, would there?" grinned one of the party.

"Would you believe me if I said 'no'?" Mark asked.

"Oh, sure," grinned the man in a tone which meant he would not. "We *all* believe you, now don't we boys?"

"As much as we believe that all Banker Snodgrass's interested in's that redheaded gal's paintings," grinned the second rancher.

"Is *that* what he told you?" inquired the South Texas lawyer. "The last one was his niece from Boston."

"Not this one," said the man who started the conversation on its present line. "Or if she is, she's the first Boston gal I ever heard that sounded like a Georgia peachblossom."

"She must be real rich, way Snodgrass took to her," grinned the rancher.

"Likely she won't stay that way when he's through," put in the youngest member of the group.

"There's time you talk too much," warned the lawyer. "Saying things like that out loud could wind you up getting called out with a gun, or hauled into a legal court."

"She sure is a real good-looking gal though," Pierce commented, watching Mark all through the conversation.

"Real good-looking," the blond giant said in a noncommittal tone. "Well, I reckon I'll be pulling out."

"Not me," Pierce drawled. "Who's for a few hands of poker?"

"Did somebody say poker?" called Bragg from the faro table "Cash me in, friend, I hear sweet music."

If there was little chance of getting the foreman away from the faro table, Mark new none at all would separate him from the kind of poker game Pierce meant to start. Still, Mark declined to play.

"I reckon I'll go to bed," he said. "You wanting to use my room, Tule?"

"At the Houston?" yelped Bragg. "That's not my kind of range. I'll see you sometime tomorrow?"

Walking from the saloon, Mark put aside all thoughts of the redheaded girl and Banker Snodgrass. Maybe Wycliffe told the truth; but if he did not and planned to avenge the insult on his family, walking the streets daydreaming would be a good way to wind up lying in the dirt and looking like a horse tromped you.

Mark's caution proved unnecessary, which did not mean he regretted showing it. From the lack of incidents he concluded that Wycliffe had carried out his promise to lead the trio out of town. Entering the imposing Houston Hotel, Mark went to the reception desk and rang the bell for the night clerk. Unlike the smaller hotels of the range country, one could not reach over and take a room key from the rack. So Mark leaned on the desk and waited. His eyes went to a large book lying closed by the ink-well. Following the growing trend in the East, and to show that Austin had risen above the status of a rough, uncurried range town, the Houston maintained a register of its guests, something likely to be regarded as showing an unnecessary inquisitiveness in most places west of the Mississippi River.

Two men entered the building and walked across to the desk. Turning the register, one of them flipped it open. Although no snob, Mark did not regard the pair as being potential Houston guests. One of them stood almost Mark's height, although without a corresponding heft, wore a derby hat, town suit, shirt, tie and boots. His face bore a tough, mocking sneer as if he felt that he did Texas a favor by being there. Studying the man, Mark noticed that the right side jacket pocket sagged as if carrying a heavy weight. Not a gun, for the bulge made was the wrong shape and he carried a light caliber Colt butt forward at his left side.

Something in the second man's attitude attracted Mark's attention. Tall, lean, dressed in range clothes, his moustached, tanned face was not that of a city dweller. Hanging in a fast-draw holster, an Army Colt showed signs of much use. The man looked Mark over from head to foot, with particular emphasis to his features. In a way it reminded the blond giant of a rancher examining a stud horse or bull and estimating its marketable value.

Another man once looked at Mark in such a manner. Remembering the circumstances, an uneasy feeling crept over him. Before he could decide what action to take, Mark saw the night clerk appear from a door behind the desk. Indignation showed on the clerk's face as he stepped hurriedly forward, spun the register back to its original position and closed it with a bang.

"Was there something?" he demanded with studied politeness.

"We want a room," the city man replied.

"Sorry. We've no vacancies."

"Maybe this'll ch————" the city man began, reaching into his jacket's inside pocket.

"Let it ride, Quigg," growled the other man, darting a glance in Mark's direction. "There's other places we can try."

For a moment Quigg seemed inclined to dispute the point, then followed the other's gaze. "Sure, Burbage, there's other places. Let's go find one."

"You want your key, Mr. Counter?" the clerk asked after the two men left.

"Why sure," Mark agreed. "Any messages?"

"None, sir. Do you want a call in the morning?"

"Not unless a telegraph message comes. Good night."

"Good night, sir."

Taking his key, Mark crossed to the stairs. Before going up, he glanced at the door and saw the two men standing outside. Neither looked back, or showed any sign of entering the building, so Mark walked upstairs and along the corridor of the first floor. Reaching room number twelve, he slipped the key into the lock and opened the door.

Instantly Mark felt something to be wrong. The room was in darkness and usually a place like the Houston left a lamp lit for its guests' benefit. Stepping forward cautiously, Mark caught a sweet aroma which most certainly had not been present when he left earlier.

The door closed of its own volition—or did it? From behind it came a soft rustling sound. While almost sure what was happening, Mark took no chances and turned toward the sound with his right hand dropping gunward. Then two arms went around his neck, a firm, yet undoubtedly feminine body pressed against him and warm lips crushed on to his mouth, kissing hard and passionately. Certain that he did not need to fear his visitor, Mark put his arms to a better use than drawing weapons and kissed back.

Freed at last from his unseen caller's grasp, he asked, "Is it all right for me to light the lamp?"

"Go to it," replied a gentle, cultured female voice.

For the first time Mark realized that more than normal night darkness caused the pitch-black condition of the room. The Houston ensured its guests' privacy by fitting thick drapes to the windows. However, the management allowed each guest to decide whether to make use of the facility. Although Mark had not drawn then before he left, they appeared to be pulled together now. Taking a match from his pocket, Mark rasped it on the seat of his pants. He found the lamp and applied the flame to its wick. Not until the lamp's light bathed the room did he offer to turn around and face his visitor.

Like all the Houston's first-floor rooms, number twelve offered more luxury than usual in Texas hotels. Facing the rear of the building, the room had a large, comfortable bed, dressing table with drawers, washstand that sported a clean white towel, and a large wardrobe.

In the center of the room stood the beautiful redheaded girl who had drawn his attention on Hood Street that afternoon. A warm, inviting smile added charm to her features as she came toward him with arms outstretched. Once more she pressed her mouth against his. Never averse to such treatment at the hands of a beautiful girl, Mark gave her an adequate reply.

"They told me this was the safest place in Austin,"

he remarked on releasing her and moving her back to arms' length.

"The lock's an ordinary lever and fitted for a master key," she replied. "I could have opened it with a bobby pin."

"I just bet you could. Say, Belle honey, I thought you'd got too high toned to speak to old friends back there on Hood Street."

"You put me in one hell of a spot, Mark," she answered in her attractive Southern drawl. "If that feller had stepped in a couple of seconds later I'd've already started getting you some help."

"Would that've been bad?" Mark asked.

"Not for you, maybe," the girl admitted. "But it would for me. Snodgrass thinks I'm a shy, unassuming lil Georgia gal with money to invest and he might've changed his mind if he heard me cussing like a trail hand hauling cows out of a mud hole."

"So you're working on Snodgrass," Mark said a touch coldly.

"Nobody else but."

"Why?"

"Because he can afford it and I figure he's asked to be trimmed for a fair piece now."

"Damn it all, Belle!" Mark began.

"Don't *you* go all high toned on me, Mark Counter!" she snapped back. "I'm a thief, but I've been one ever since you met me and never pretended to be anything else but one to you."

"A nice gal like you doesn't have to be one," he growled.

"No," the girl agreed. "I could go back home and marry off to some rancher. Grow old before my time raising kids and watching him sweat out his guts to make a decent spread from a strip of beat-up range. See every red cent he makes go into the bank to pay off interest on a mortgage and then, just when it looks like he's going to make it, have the bank foreclose and run him off."

"That's what happened to your folks, huh?" Mark said gently.

"Sure. Paw struggled to keep the place going through the War. Sold cattle to the Army—only they paid him in Confederate money. Then after it ended—well, you saw what happened."

"I was luckier than most; pappy kept his money in gold, not paper."

"So did my paw, what he had, put it into a real safe place too. A bank. Only the bank failed. The new feller who took it on sounded real helpful, lending us and our neighbors money to keep going. Only he stopped being helpful before we could pay him back."

"The law didn't help?"

"What law? Davis' lousy state police? It was them who ran us off our spread. I swore I'd make that banker sweat and did."

"His name's not Snodgrass," Mark pointed out.

"They're so alike you'd think the same father spawned them," Belle snorted. "I'm no saint, Mark. And I'm not the James boys making out that I rob the rich to give to the poor. But I've never yet robbed a man who didn't ask for it."

Coming to a halt, with her heated tirade, the girl stared half-defiantly at the blond giant. Looking back, a smile played on Mark's lips, but he felt a little sad too. Ever since their meeting the previous year he had felt a strong attraction for the beautiful lady outlaw, Belle Starr.* A spirited, gay girl, she had a zest for life which set her apart from any other women he had ever met. The only one who came close being Calamity Jane, and Mark regarded her in a very different manner. Where he thought of

* Told in *Troubled Range*.

Calamity almost in the light of a tomboy sister, he regarded Belle as a woman—and what a woman.

"It's your life," he told the girl.

"Thanks for not preaching at me," she replied. "There's no sound so sweet to me as the screech of a banker when he's been plucked. I tell you, Mark, there's nothing I like better than making one screech."

"Nothing?" Mark repeated.

"In the way of business, I mean," Belle answered and looked pointedly across the room. "You never did finish teaching me to play poker."

For the first time, following the direction of the girl's gaze, Mark noticed a boxed deck of cards lying on the bed's covers. Crossing the room, he sat on one side of the bed. After unbucking his gunbelt and placing it on the dressing table, he took up the cards. Thumbing open the box, he slid out the pasteboards and then raised his eyes to Belle's smiling face as she sat at the other side.

"Come to think of it," he said, "I never did at that. The first thing we have to do is shuffle the deck."

"Is it?" asked the girl innocently.

"Sure is."

"But it might take all night for us to—finish the game."

"Darned if I'd've thought of that," Mark grinned. "Only according to Hoyle———"

"A feller I know says that Hoyle never played poker in his whole life," Belle objected. "Anyway, what right's some limey got to tell us red-blooded Americans how we should play cards?"

"You've convinced me," Mark grinned and dealt out two hands.

"I'll open with a pair of shoes," Belle remarked, without picking up her cards.

Half an hour later, after an instructive period of

betting and raising, the lesson had ended. Darkness once more filled the room.

"Why'd you rescue that lobby-lizzie on Hood Street?" asked Belle's voice. "You could've got hurt and then I'd never have learned how to play poker."

"It seemed like a good idea at the time," Mark replied.

"She looked like she'd've liked nothing better than walk off on your arm."

"I was a mite disappointed when she didn't," grinned Mark.

"What'd she got that I haven't?" demanded Belle.

"Nothing," admitted Mark. "And a whole heap less of it."

"Flattery will get you a long way, young man," purred the lady outlaw. "As long as you don't spend all night talking about it."

"I always figured to be a man of action, not words," Mark told her.

"Then act," Belle replied.

CHAPTER FOUR

A Lady Outlaw in Distress

MARK stirred in the bed as he heard a pounding on his door. While the room remained dark, he could see daylight through a small gap in the curtains. Sitting up, he called, "Who is it?"

"You're expecting maybe Robert E. Lee?" Tule Bragg's rasping voice answered. "Rise up, boy and let a tired ole man inside."

Which, in view of how Mark had spent the night, could prove a mite embarrassing. Then he realized that he had the room to himself. Reaching out his left hand, he touched only the sheets and he made out the empty shape of the pillow, sunken by a head's pressure, at his side. Swinging his feet to the ground, Mark sat up and reached for his pants, looked around and found no trace of his visitor of the previous night.

"She sure moves soft and easy," he mused, drawing on the pants, "in more ways than one."

Suddenly he remembered that he did not mention the two men to Belle. Yet he wondered if their business might be connected with her. On the first time he met Belle, a bounty hunter called Framant had been after her. When Framant came on Mark in the Elkhorn livery barn, he looked the Texan over in the same way that Burbage had, calculatingly, trying to see if his face struck a note from a wanted poster.

Hunting wanted men for the price on their heads had been the way Framant made his living. Burbage too, or Mark missed his guess.

Deciding that he would give Belle a warning at the earliest opportunity, Mark walked across to the door and unlocked it. He knew something of the girl's skill at opening locked doors and felt no surprise to find it secured as it had been before they finished their game of poker.

Bragg leaned against the door jamb, unshaven and yet showing no sign of having missed a night's sleep.

"Afternoon," he greeted laconically, although the time was no more than half past nine in the morning.

"How'd it go?" Mark growled inhospitably, allowing the foreman to enter.

"Could've been worse. I come out a lil mite ahead."

"Which means you've won a bundle and won't stop bragging about it all week."

"You boys at the OD Connected sure live well, happen this's the time of day you get up," drawled Bragg, crossing the room and pulling open the curtains. "And I never got to boasting about my winnings. Say though, talking about that, there was this time down in Amarillo back in '58———"

"There I sat, two lil deuces showing and nothing in the hole," Mark interrupted. "And him with two pairs kings riding high."

"Have I told you about it afore?" inquired Bragg in a surprised tone.

"Not more'n twenty-thirty times, I'd say," Mark replied and scowled as the foreman began to sniff the air. "Now what's wrong?"

Wrinkling his nose in an expression of disgust, Bragg crossed the room. He drew apart the curtains and unfastened and raised the bottom part of the window.

"Figure to clear the air a mite," he explained.

"Way this room smells, the cleaning gal might get the wrong idea, or the right one; and I'm damned if I know which'd be worse."

"To each his own," drawled Mark tolerantly. "You like gambling and I don't."

"Neither did I when I was your age," grunted Bragg. "I'm hungry."

"We'll get a shave in the barber shop downstairs and then have some breakfast," Mark suggested as he dressed.

"Damned if I'd pay the sort of prices they ask for a room and let 'em make me shave afore I eat," the foreman drawled. "Anyways, in a fancy place like this, I thought they'd make you have a shave afore they let you into the barber shop."

All through his shave and while eating breakfast, Mark tried to decide what he should do about Belle Starr's presence in town. To some people the answer would have been clear: warn the banker. Mark did not see it that way. All too well he remembered the conditions during Reconstruction when "liberal" bigots sought to smash down those who dared oppose their lofty ideals and carpetbagger scum used official positions to loot and rob. Many an otherwise honest Texan had been driven into a life of crime at that time. Maybe Mark would have been under different circumstances. There were personal loyalties involved too. A man like Mark Counter did not easily turn his back on a friend.

Refusing Bragg's offer to go along and help with his father's business, Mark walked the streets of the city and tried to solve his problem. From the comments made by the young man at the Bigfoot the previous night, Snodgrass might deserve plucking. Reaching a decision, Mark turned his steps toward the office of a prominent lawyer. As the lawyer was also his uncle, Mark gained admission with no difficulty. After talking over different subjects,

Mark brought up the subject of Snodgrass' character. Always a forthright man, his uncle left him in no doubt that the young man's views had been correct. The lawyer refrained from asking any questions as to Mark's reason for making the inquiry and the meeting ended as amiably as it had begun.

By the time Mark reached the street, he decided to let things ride. When he suggested she forget the whole deal, during the previous night, Belle insisted that other people were too deeply involved for her to back out and leave them. One thing Mark felt sure of. With Belle planning and organizing things, there would be no violence involved. He also felt willing to bet that she'd arranged things to ensure no innocent person would suffer through the robbery.

Having made his decision, Mark gave thought to his horse. He knew that Belle rented a room on his floor at the hotel, although on the other side of the passage, but did not intend to go to see her. While intending to remain impassive in the affair, he also felt that any further contact between them must come to some other town. So he went to the livery barn where he left his huge blood bay stallion on arrival in Austin. Everything necessary for the horse's well-being was attended to by the time Mark arrived and he knew the rest would do it good. On checking, he found one of the blood bay's shoes needed replacing and went to attend to the matter.

With his horse reshod, Mark returned to the hotel. He found a message from Bragg warning that the business would take longer than expected, but no word from Ole Devil. Dining alone in the hotel, he felt bored and decided he would head for San Garcia after seeing Sailor Sam. Maybe Dusty did not need help, but anything beat hanging around Austin unless he had his friends with him.

Like most men who often spent long periods with little sleep, Mark had developed the habit of grabbing some when the opportunity arose. Going to his room, he removed hat, boots and gunbelt, lay on the bed and drifted almost immediately to a deep sleep.

Night had fallen when Mark woke. Sitting on the bed, he looked around the room and then came to his feet. Crossing the room, he opened the door with the intention of looking for one of the hotel staff to ask for water. Then he heard voices on the stairs.

"It's room seven, gentlemen," came the fruity tones of the night clerk. "I can't say that I approve————"

Mark drew the door until it was nearly closed at the words. Standing in the darkness, he peered through the slit and listened to a conversation he knew to be private. Room number seven across and along the passage was rented by Belle Starr, under the name "Magnolia Beauregard."

"You're not paid to approve or disapprove," said a hard, clipped New England accent. "That letter I showed you said for you to give us every cooperation."

"Is she up there now?" asked a second Eastern voice as the night clerk appeared in Mark's range of vision.

"She hasn't handed in her key if she's gone out," replied the hotel man.

The other two speakers came into sight. One of them Mark recognized as the dude who showed such an interest in the hotel register the previous night. At his side walked another obvious dude. Not quite so tall, but with a powerful build, he dressed in better taste than his companion. Much the same kind of gunbelt hung under the man's city jacket, a pearl-handled Smith & Wesson No. 2 revolver in its cross-draw holster. At .32 caliber, despite its manufacturer's calling it an "Army" revolver, the gun did not impress Mark. He had been reared in the Texas tradition that even .36 was a touch light in caliber when one's life depended on it. Handsome but hard as nails was the way the man struck Mark, studying him through the crack in the doorway.

Moving around cautiously, Mark watched the three men halt before the door marked "7." Either the two dudes did not regard Belle as dangerous, or they lacked training in certain basic peace officer matters. Flanking the clerk as he knocked on the door, they would have been in the line of fire should the room's occupant start throwing lead. That did not happen, nor did the door open. After a moment the second dude looked at the clerk.

"Use your passkey."

"It's on your head if anything goes wrong," warned the clerk as he obeyed.

Once again Mark marveled at men whom he imagined to be peace officers, acting in such a suicidal manner. Neither of them took the precaution of drawing a gun as they entered the room. Then they walked out again, alone.

"She's not there," Quigg growled.

"Our guests occasionally take their keys with them when they leave," the clerk pointed out. "The cleaning staff have passkeys———"

"I've got the bank covered," interrupted the other dude. "In case she comes back, I'll wait in the hall. You'd best stay here, Quigg."

"Sure, Mr. Shafto. You want for me to wait in the passage?"

"In her room, damnit! If you hang around in the hall, somebody'll see you and start yelling for the manager."

"I'm not sure that———" began the clerk.

"You don't have to be sure of anything!" Shafto barked. "I'll handle any complaints. Go on in, Quigg."

Mark felt as if a cold hand touched him as he

watched Quigg enter Belle's room. While he did not know what kind of lawman Shafto might be, he felt that he could hazard a pretty fair guess. Certainly he was no Western-trained peace officer, that showed in the lack of precautions taken at the door to Belle's room. In the early 1870s there was no national law enforcement office, it all being managed at state level. Even the U.S. Secret Service concerned itself only with forgers and counterfeiters. As Belle only operated in the West, she could not have fallen afoul of Eastern lawmen, except for one kind. It could even be debated that the men involved had no official standing, if the point arose.

After retiring from the command of the U.S. Secret Service at the end of the Civil War, Allan Pinkerton had organized his own private detective agency. Using the methods employed with varying success against the South's efficient spy networks, Pinkerton worked for banks, railroads and other big business combines to stamp out the enormous crime wave which rose with the uneasy peace. Unless Mark missed badly in his guess, Shafto, Quigg and Burbage belonged to the Pinkerton Agency; the former pair being regular operatives and the latter hired for local knowledge.

If the men had belonged to an official law enforcement agency, Mark would have been faced with the serious problem of his future actions. He felt no such responsibility where Pinkerton's men were concerned. Like most Southerners, Mark disliked Allan Pinkerton and regarded his agency with suspicion. Not for another eighteen or more months would come the "bomb incident," when Pinkerton agents threw either a bomb or a harmless "Grecian-fire" flare into the home of Jesse James' parents to kill the outlaw's eight-year-old half-brother and blow his mother's right arm off; but every man who served the Confederacy remembered ugly rumors of Southern prisoners-of-war being tortured by the Yankee Secret Service under the flimsy pretense of extracting information. So Mark felt no compunctions about helping Belle to avoid falling into Shafto's clutches. From the little Mark saw of the man, he guessed any prisoner with information would be worked on to be induced to part with it.

Crossing to his bed, Mark dressed quickly. As he reached the door, he remembered that the window, opened by Bragg that morning, was not closed. Although the room overlooked a wide alley and the rear of a line of business premises, he doubted if anybody could reach its window without the aid of a ladder. Even if they did, there was little that could be stolen. When heading for Tennyson, he'd traveled light and had only taken a change of clothes in addition to spare ammunition. The big wardrobe held only a few garments unlikely to fit the average sneak-thief and his rifle. He had left his heavy, low-horned, double-girthed saddle hanging on a burro in the locked room at the livery barn. So Mark left the window open, stepped into the passage and locked the door. He could hear Shafto and the clerk talking as he walked down the stairs.

"I can't hardly believe it," the clerk wailed. "Miss Beauregard's been————"

"You don't have to believe anything," Shafto put in. "And don't let out a peep to anybody about what we're doing here. I'll stay in the lobby here until she comes back. Is there another way in?"

"Only through the rear door and up the service stairs at the back."

"You go and watch there, Burbage," ordered Shafto and darted a glance to where Mark stepped into view at the bottom of the stairs.

"Good evening, Mr. Counter," greeted the clerk. "Do you wish to hand your key in?"

"Sure," Mark replied, doing so. "No word from Ole Devil yet?"

"None. Where will you be if it comes?"

"It's likely to be anyplace. I couldn't make a start tonight anyway."

With that Mark turned and walked out of the front door. As he went, he could feel the men's eyes on him. Crossing the street, he stood for a moment and tried to decide how he might best find Belle to give a warning of her danger. From what he heard, the men appeared to expect her attempt to be made that night. So he made his way through the town until reaching the street on which Snodgrass' bank was situated. Fortunately enough people used the street for Mark to stroll along in a reasonable crowd. Having worked as a lawman both in a tough Montana gold town and on the Rio Hondo ranges, Mark could guess what kind of arrangements Shafto had made. As he walked along, his eyes darted constantly around. He saw three obvious members of Shafto's defending force, looking just too casual propping up walls to a trained eye. There would be more at the rear of the bank. Much as he hated to admit it, Mark saw that Shafto had been thorough. Any attempt to rob the bank that night was doomed to failure.

For a time Mark waited in a small saloon, watching the bank. Then he decided to return to the hotel. If he located the waiting Pinkerton men, Belle would be no less successful. So she would either postpone or call off her robbery.

While walking along the street toward the Houston, Mark saw a shape emerge from a side alley in front of him. Although a hooded cloak effectively concealed the shape's face and figure, Mark felt sure enough of her identity to stride forward in her direction.

"Belle!" he said.

Turning, the lady outlaw reached her right hand into the top of her reticule. Then she brought it out empty, although Mark guessed that her Manhattan Navy revolver rode in the special holster which prevented its presence being detected.

"Hi, Mark," she greeted.

"Let's get off the street," he growled, taking her arm and steering her back into the alley.

"What's wrong?" she asked, suddenly realizing that he called her by her name instead of using her alias.

"There're Pinkertons waiting at the hotel and watching the bank."

If Mark expected to create a sensation with his words, he failed. Not that he expected the girl to show too much emotion, but he felt the news ought to have come as something of a surprise. Instead, all she did was nod her head gravely.

"I figured they'd be covering the bank," she admitted. "But not the hotel. Are you sure it's me they're after?"

"They asked for your room and there's one of them in it right now."

"Damnation!" Belle snorted. "If I thought that——"

"What?" prompted Mark. "Do you reckon somebody snitched on you?"

"Somebody must have," agreed Belle.

"Me?"

Gently she took his powerful hands in her own, raised herself on to tiptoes and kissed him lightly on the lips. "You'd be the last one I'd think it of. No, Mark, I've an idea who sold me."

"You'd best get out of town," Mark told her.

"Sure. But there're a few things I must get from the hotel. A change of clothes, things like that."

"One of them's in your room, like I said," warned Mark.

"If I sneak in the back way———" the girl began.

"Nary a chance, gal. There's a hard-eyed jasper called Burbage watching the back door and another in the front lobby."

"That sounds like Dick Shafto's work. He's thorough and one man I wouldn't want to have laying hands on me. But I have to get into my room. I can't get away dressed like this."

"That's for sure," Mark said, catching a glimpse of a décolleté silk dress under her cloak. "How'd you plan to leave happen everything went all right?"

"By stage," Belle explained. "But I've a good horse waiting in case I had to break for the tall timber. That means wearing something a whole heap more suitable than this frock."

"You can walk on in through either the front or back door and I'll be right behind to see you're not stopped," Mark told her.

"And after you've done it?" she asked.

"Let me worry about after."

Slowly Belle shook her head, and squeezed his hands. "No, Mark. You're not breaking the law to help me."

"We'd be together."

"When we get together, it won't be so we have to watch our back-trail and run every time a stranger looks sideways at us."

A plan began to form in Mark's head, one which could work. If it did, Belle would have the chance to collect her property. While the plan had more than a little risk, with the chance of him ending up on the run from the law, Mark decided to put it into practice.

"I reckon I can get you into the hotel without being seen," he said. "After that———"

"I'll play the hand out my own way," Belle stated. "Don't argue, Mark. It's the only way I'll go along with you."

"You're a determined woman, Miss Starr," he

said and kissed her. "Now let's get the hell from here."

With that Mark took the girl's arm and led her to the rear of the alley. Keeping to the back streets, they reached the Houston, not on the street at the front, but in the darkened area behind the building. Watching how Mark looked up at the first floor windows, Belle guessed partly at what he meant to do. For all that, she felt a touch surprised when he came to a halt below his room. Placing his back to the wall, he bowed his legs slightly, cupped his hands together and held them before him.

"You're figuring to hoist me up *there*?" she asked. "So I can go through the window into your room."

"If it's not my room, there's likely to be some screaming," Mark replied. "I left the window open and it's the only one that is."

Stepping forward, Belle raised her right foot and placed it in his hands. She threw the cloak back over her shoulders and nodded. "Ready!" she said, then smiled. "No peeking, mind."

"Why'd I need to peek? grinned Mark. "Get set. Shove up!"

Obediently Belle forced down with her left leg and felt herself rising into the air under the thrust of Mark's arms. Higher she rose until her feet reached the level of his chest.

"I'll have to go up still more!" she warned.

Mark guessed that and changed his hold. Carefully he eased his hands apart, one under each of Belle's shoes. Sucking in a breath, he continued to raise her upward. Resting her hands on the wall, Belle stretched above her head. She felt the window ledge and her fingers closed over it.

"I'm almost there!" she hissed. "Just a little higher."

At which point a man came from the shadows of the next building and walked toward them.

CHAPTER FIVE

A Mistake Anybody Could Make

NEVER had Mark felt so completely at a disadvantage as he did when he saw the shape walking toward him from the blackness of the next building. The surrounding darkness prevented him from doing more than identify the approaching figure as being male; he could see nothing to tell him who the other might be. Nor could he think of any acceptable reason for his actions when the newcomer started to ask the obvious questions. Supporting the girl above him at arms' length, Mark could not draw a weapon. If he removed one hand, always assuming he could hold Belle's weight on the other, it was doubtful if she would be able to keep her balance.

Drawing a gun was no answer, and Mark knew it. While he wished to help the girl escape, he would not do so at the cost of another man's life. Even if the newcomer proved to be a Pinkerton man reporting to Shafto, Mark doubted whether he could kill the other. Besides which, the sound of the shot would bring Burbage out to investigate.

Before any solution presented itself to Mark, or Belle—and, to give her credit, her first instinct was to warn him not to shoot the new arrival—the man spoke.

"You-all should use the kind of hotel I do, boy,"

came Bragg's drawling voice. "Then you wouldn't have to sneak the gal in."

Relief flooded over Mark at the sound of his old friend's tones. "Damn you, Tule," he growled. "Kind of place you stop in, they'd not expect you to sneak anything but a pig inside."

"Not even that," said Bragg cheerfully. "You should hear 'em grunting in the room next to mine. You all right up there, ma'am?"

"Apart from being scared white-haired, I'm fine!" Belle gritted, realizing that she did not need to worry about the man below betraying her. "Hold firm just a mite longer, Mark."

With that she started to shove up the window section as high as it would go. Cursing the dress and cloak, although she knew that Snodgrass would never have accepted her as a *bona fide* rich, naive Southern belle had she visited him dressed in the kind of clothing the present situation called for, she began to pull herself into Mark's room. Cloth ripped, shapely legs waved wildly and a number of unladylike comments broke from Belle before she slid through the window. She landed in an undignified roll learned when coming off a horse's back involuntarily during her rearing-years on the ranch. Rising, she looked out of the window at the two men and waved a cheery hand.

"I'm all right."

"Wait until I come up there," Mark replied in as low a voice as he could manage with the hope of the girl hearing him but not the waiting man in the hotel. "Do it, gal. I've got a jim-dandy idea for getting your gear. And without needing to shoot up any of that Pinkerton bunch."

"Dang it, and I figured you to be eloping," Bragg said as the girl ducked back into the room. "Or have her folks set the Pink-eyes on your trail?"

"Something like that," Mark agreed, turning to

walk toward the corner of the building. "You game to help me bust the law a mite, Tule?"

"I'm game. Figured there was something wrong when I saw you haul the gal into the alley back there. Got to thinking and remembered how you looked at her back on Hood Street yesterday. I'd've sworn then you recognized her and thought she'd speak. That's mighty sweet-smelling perfume she uses, boy, if it does linger just a lil mite. So I tagged along just in case."

"You allow I'd fallen for the old badger game, or something?"

"I don't know what I reckoned, but I allowed to be on hand should you need some help."

"Which same I need," Mark admitted.

"That figures," Bragg replied.

"The gal's Belle Starr and the Pink-eyes are waiting to grab her."

"Boy, I wronged you for sure when I thought you might be heading for trouble," the foreman stated soberly. "Yes sirree, bub, I was sure wrong."

"Was, huh?" grunted Mark unsympathetically.

"Yep. You're not in trouble. It's just that the water's up over the willows and your swimming hoss died," drawled the foreman, mentioning one of the hazards a cowhand on a trail herd met in the form of a river running in full flood. "Let's go get her out. Damned stinking Yankee Pink-eyes!"

"We'll do that," Mark promised as they reached the street and turned along the front of the hotel. "Only we do it this way."

With that he quickly explained the new version of his plan. Bragg's presence allowed Mark more scope and made his idea more practical than before. Although the foreman snorted and growled a curse when hearing of the Pinkerton agent in Belle's room, he admitted that Mark's plan ought to work given just a smidgin of Texas good fortune.

"Anyways, you'll have a mighty good reason for jumping him," Bragg continued cheerfully.

"Things could go wrong," Mark pointed out. "If they do, we'll have trouble."

"Day I start worrying about trouble, I'm going to quit working for you fool Counters and go live with my sister back East," Bragg answered. "The hell with the Pink-eyes. Who the hell do they reckon they are, coming to Texas and abusing honest folks this ways?"

While a moralist might have pointed out that Belle Starr did not come under the category of "honest folks," Mark let the matter ride. Comforted by the knowledge that he had a loyal friend at his side, the blond giant led the way into the hotel. Seated to one side of the front entrance, Shafto lowered the newspaper he pretended to be reading for long enough to look at Mark and Bragg. Then he raised it once again and gave the impression of being engrossed in the latest Austin happenings. Discussing the likelihood of Sailor Sam arriving the following morning, Mark and the foreman crossed the lobby and halted at the desk. After collecting his key and asking for any messages, Mark led Bragg upstairs.

On entering his room, Mark found that Belle had not wasted her time. While she still wore the cloak, her dress lay in a neatly folded pile on the bed. Guessing what the cloak concealed, Mark almost wished that Bragg was not on his heels. Belle looked calm and unruffled despite having climbed through the window and undressed quickly. Smiling from Mark to Bragg, she looked expectantly back at the big blond.

"You see, I waited," she said.

"If you hadn't, I'd've caught you and paddled your hide," Mark replied. "I put a heap of thinking into getting you out of here."

"Thinking don't come easy to them Counters,

ma'am,'' Bragg went on. "I'm Tule Bragg, his
pappy's foreman.''

"Mark's told me about you," smiled Belle.

"It's lies, every danged word of it!'' Bragg insisted, then became sober. "You ready, boy?''

"Passage's clear, let's give it a whirl,'' Mark
replied. "We're going to haul that jasper out of your
room, Belle gal.''

"No———!'' she began.

"Boy's got a real tricky lil idea worked out,
ma'am,'' Bragg put in.

"Has he told you who you're helping and why?''

"Yep. Not that he needed to tell me; there's only
one Belle Starr.''

"You'll be making me blush next," she said and
turned to Mark. "How do you plan to do it?''

Mark told her and she nodded in agreement. Not
only did the plan stand a good chance of working,
but it offered Mark and Bragg a passable excuse for
their actions. Certainly the new scheme sounded
safer than Mark's original idea. So any objections
she might have felt died away. Her chief concern had
been for Mark's fate after she made her escape,
knowing the vindictive nature of her hunters. If
everything went smoothly, the worst light Mark
could be regarded in was for acting a touch hastily.

"Go to it,'' she said.

"We're on our way,'' Mark replied.

For all that, only Bragg walked along the deserted
corridor toward Belle's room. Mark remained at the
door of number twelve and Belle stood out of sight
behind the door. While waiting for the men to join
her, she had drawn the curtains to prevent any
chance of being seen from outside. Everything
depended on how the man in her room acted.

Coming to number seven, Bragg drew close to the
door and turned its handle. He heard a scuffling
sound from inside and pressed his ear against the

panel. For a short time nothing happened, then he
detected stealthy footsteps approaching inside the
room. Swiftly and silently the foreman glided along
the passage and around a corner out of sight of
Belle's door.

Slowly the door to Belle's room opened and
Quigg's head emerged. He looked toward the corner
around which Bragg disappeared. Acting as if he had
just arrived and was letting himself into his quarters,
Mark coughed. Just as Mark hoped would happen,
Quigg swung to look his way and then ducked back
into the room. To a casual observer the man's actions
would have appeared highly suspicious, one of the
things Mark counted on happening.

Darting along the passage, Mark dropped his
shoulder and charged the door. The Houston had
been built to last, its rooms far more soundproof
than those of most hotels in Texas and its doors
stoutly constructed. Struck by two hundred pounds
of driving muscle and sinew, the door still burst
open. Standing just behind it, Quigg saw his danger
too late. The door swung inward, catching him and
sending him sprawling across the room. He hit the
wardrobe, which halted his progress and saw the
blond giant enter.

Once again Quigg acted as Mark wanted him to
do. Spluttering a curse, the dude stabbed his right
hand into the sagging pocket. While most western
men would have reached for their gun, Mark figured
that Quigg went for a weapon he understood better
than a firearm. Anyway, Quigg's action gave Mark
the excuse he wanted.

Bounding across the room, even as a wicked
leather-wrapped, lead-loaded billy whipped from
Quigg's pocket, Mark ripped a punch into the man's
belly. The billy fell from Quigg's hand as he grabbed
at his middle and doubled over. Up came Mark's
other hand in a driving blow that caught the dude's

offered chin with smooth precision. Lifted erect by
the blow, Quigg smashed into the wardrobe again.
His legs buckled under him and he collapsed as if he
had been suddenly boned.

"Neat," said Bragg at the door. "Nobody's
showing themselves."

"Get Belle here *pronto*," Mark replied, kneeling
by Quigg and making sure he could not hear or see
anything.

Not until Bragg left to obey the order did Mark
find time to look around the room. It seemed that
Quigg had spent his time searching Belle's property,
for every drawer had been turned out and her clothes
lay in a pile on the floor of the wardrobe. Hearing the
rapid patter of feet, Mark turned and saw the girl enter. Annoyance flashed on her face as she studied the
condition of her belongings, then she gave a chuckle.

"Much good that did him," she said.

"Is anything missing?" Mark asked.

"There was nothing for him to steal," she replied.
"And he didn't look in the right place for the things
that matter."

Going to the bed, she drew away the covers until
she exposed the mattress. Like all the other Houston
fixtures, it offered the guest plenty of comfort; being
thick and well packed. Collecting a pair of scissors
from the workbasket Quigg upended in his search for
evidence, Belle cut open the stitching at the bottom
of the mattress. Reaching into the slit she made, the
girl drew out a man's shirt and Levi's pants. She then
carefully closed the gap and rapidly remade the bed.
All the time she worked, Mark stood guard over the
unconscious Pinkerton agent and Bragg remained at
the door, watching the passage.

"Move it, Belle," Mark said. "He won't be out
much longer and I don't want to have to hit him
again."

"All right," she replied, darting to the wardrobe

and taking out a pair of riding boots "That's all I need. My gunbelt, saddle and hat're with friends."

"How about the rest of your stuff?" asked Bragg, indicating a velvet-lined box which stood open on the dressing table and showing several items of apparently costly jewelery.

"That can stay here," Belle answered. "It's not real and the clothes were bought for this job. If I leave them, it will give me a start."

"They'll not know you've been back," Bragg admitted.

A low moan from Quigg warned them of the need for movement. Holding the clothes and boots, Belle left the room and headed toward Mark's quarters. Waiting until the girl entered and closed the door, the two men hoisted Quigg up between them and hauled him out, then along toward the stairs.

Throwing off her cloak, Belle stood clad in a brief set of underclothes which would have aroused Banker Snodgrass' suspicions had he been privileged to see them. Not that he would have found anything to complain at in the way she filled the flimsy silk. Kicking off her shoes, she retained the black stockings which showed her magnificent legs to their best advantage and donned the trousers. Next she drew on the shirt, tucking it into the pants and buttoning it up. The riding boots came next. Belle drew them on, snuggling her feet into the comforting touch of the stout leather. Then she thrust the Manhattan revolver from her reticule into the waistband of her pants. With a sigh of content, she knew that she could now make good her escape.

A coiled rope hung on a peg fixed to the side of the wardrobe. Modern in many ways, the Houston still retained the traditional Western style of fire precautions. Taking the rope, Belle doused the lamp and went to the window. She drew back the curtains and looked out. Satisfied that nobody watched the rear of the building, she slipped the honda of the rope over the hook stoutly fastened to the wall and tossed the other end out. Then she gathered her property, wrapping the cloak around her dress and shoes. At the window, she let the bundle fall and waited to see if its soft thud attracted any attention. When it did not, she climbed from the window and slid rapidly to the ground.

"Thanks for everything, big feller," she breathed, looking up at the window. "I'll never forget this."

Her chance to repay Mark would come much sooner than she imagined.

Hearing the thud of feet on the stairs, Shafto started to lower his newspaper to take a surreptitious glance. When he saw Mark and Bragg hauling Quigg down between them, he lost his casual air. Crumpling the paper, he threw it aside and came to his feet. Behind the reception desk, the clerk stared with bug-out eyes and a mouth that hung wide open.

"Get the marshal here," Mark ordered in a loud voice as he and Bragg let their groaning burden drop ungently to the floor. "We caught this jasper robbing a lady's room."

"But—but he's a———!" spluttered the clerk.

"Go fetch the marshal, son." Bragg told a gaping bellhop who came loping up. "They do say this town's so plumb law-abiding that a feller has to ask real polite afore he shoots a thieving son-of-a-bitch."

"There's no call to do that," Shafto growled, coming to the desk.

"You wouldn't say that had you seen the sneaky way this *hombre* ducked back inside the lady's room when he saw us coming," Bragg replied, stirring the moaning Quigg with his toe. Then suspicion glowed on the foreman's face and he took on the attitude of a country bumpkin in the big city for the first time. "Maybe you're in it with him, feller."

"I am, in a manner of speaking," Shafto agreed

and started to reach for his inside breast pocket.

He stopped, frozen immobile by the barrel of Bragg's big Dance ramming into his favorite belly.

"Don't you-all try it!" the foreman warned. "I've allus heard you city jaspers are mighty tricky."

"Damn it!" Shafto yelled at the clerk. "Tell them who I am!"

"This's Mr. Shafto of the Pinkerton Detective Agency," the clerk announced, trying to sound as if it was not his fault. "That's one of his men."

"You should try paying your help better, mister," Mark said as Bragg thrust away the Dance.

"Huh!" grunted the startled Shafto.

"We found in him that pretty young lady's room and from the way her gear was thrown around, he'd been robbing her."

"He was waiting there to arrest her!" Shafto snarled, kneeling at Quigg's side. "Did you have to rough-handle him this bad?"

"I'd say 'yes' to that," Mark replied calmly. "When I got to her door, I didn't knock polite and shout, 'Hey, are you-all in there robbing the lady.' I went in fast."

"And when that Jasper started reaching for his pocket, ole Mark didn't reckon he was looking for his wipe," Bragg went on. "Which same that *hombre* can reckon he come off lucky. There's some who would've shot him first and apologized when they found that all he wanted was his handkerchief."

Shafto looked at the two men in cold anger, yet he thought only that pure accident caused the disruption of his plans. Any man born in the range country, where gunhandling was taught as a matter of simple self-preservation, would have acted in the same way under the circumstances. Only, as Bragg had said, many would not have restricted themselves to merely knocking Quigg unconscious when he had tried to produce the wicked billy Shafto knew he carried.

Before any more could be said, the front door burst open and a disheveled, red-faced Banker Snodgrass charged in. Mark could never remember seeing a man look so all-fired, out-and-out furious as Snodgrass did as he bore down on the Pinkerton agent. An expression of almost sick realization began to creep over Shafto's features, as if he could guess what was coming.

"Shafto!" Snodgrass howled. "Just what kind of fool game are you playing?"

"What's happened?" countered the detective.

"Damnit, I pay your agency a retainer to be protected and I expect value for my money, sir!"

"But what——"

"You come to see me with the tale that my bank's going to be robbed. So I allow you every facility, let you bring in men that I'll have to pay for—and what, I say *what* happens?"

"Maybe you'd best tell me," Shafto growled.

"I've every intention of telling you, sir!" screeched the banker. "While all this high-priced help that I don't aim to pay for are sitting watching my bank, my house is robbed."

"Your house?" gulped Shafto.

"My house, sir. MY HOME!" Snodgrass went on. "As I returned to discover."

Shafto's mouth dropped open, then clamped home in a tight line. Watching the Pinkerton agent, Mark could see him making an almost visible attempt to rally under the shock. Despite the blond giant's antipathy, he could not help admiring the manner in which Shafto regained control of himself. Standing at the desk, the detective glared down at the moaning, writhing Quigg, then looked at the clerk.

"Get Burbage from the back!" Shafto ordered. "I'll go with you in a minute, Mr. Snodgrass."

"Go to it," the clerk said and the bellhop took a reluctant departure.

"What's up?" asked Burbage, coming from the rear of the building. Then he skidded to a halt and stared at Quigg. "Who————"

"I'll explain later," interrupted Shafto. "Go up to her room and wait in case she comes back."

"Sure. What happened to Quigg?"

"Forget him, damnit. And make sure that *you* stop in the room so nobody sees you."

Then Burbage guessed what had happened and a broad grin creased his face. Hired temporarily for his local knowledge, he had so far found the smug, big-city condescension shown him by his employers annoying. It seemed that they were not so smart after all. Quigg must have been seen looking out of the girl's room and was jumped by the two cowhands who took him for a thief.

It was a mistake anybody could make. Yet Burbage began to get an uneasy feeling that something went wrong in it. Realizing that he would have to stay on the alert while dealing with a smart, range-bred girl like Belle Starr, Burbage put out of his head the nagging, all but forgotten something which pricked at him.

After Burbage went to take over his new lookout post, Quigg had been taken into the clerk's office, and Shafto had accompanied Snodgrass to the scene of the crime, Mark went back to his room with Bragg.

"The lil devil," the foreman said with an admiring grin as he pulled in and coiled the rope. "She pulled the damned job after all—and in a way that only Snodgrass could get hurt."

"Him and Pinkerton's bunch," corrected Mark. "They won't forget it, Tule."

CHAPTER SIX

The Death of a Friend

NEXT morning all Austin buzzed with talk of the robbery. Although almost every outlaw band in the state received credit for looting Snodgrass' safe, the Pinkerton agents did not announce Belle's part in it. That did not surprise Mark. Most people in Texas knew that the girl only robbed people who deserved, by their treatment of others, to be trimmed. Probably Snodgrass demanded that the identity of his robber be held back. He had suffered a heavy personal loss, and his ego was badly bruised, but felt things could be far worse. If folks learned that Belle Starr had robbed him, they might easily fight shy of depositing or leaving their money in his care. Maybe Shafto would not have been so compliant if he had not objected to people knowing that a woman had outsmarted him.

When the girl apparently did not return to collect her property, Shafto gathered his men and went out of town looking for her. The sheriff of Travis County offered to lend the services of his posse, but Shafto declined. So two groups of men rode from the state capital to scour the surrounding district in search of some sign of Belle's passing.

Mark spent a quiet morning, although he could not help wondering how soon it would be before Shafto heard of the slit-open mattress in Belle's room and began to get suspicious.

After attending to his horse, Mark paid a delayed courtesy call to the governor. In addition to being the man appointed to clear up the mess left by Davis' corrupt administration, Stanton Howard was a friend of both Mark's father and Ole Devil Hardin. So he would have regarded Mark's nonarrival as a slight. Explaining that he figured Howard had enough on hand without entertaining every drifting cowhand, Mark excused himself for not appearing sooner or attending a formal visit at the governor's mansion. They discussed state affairs, including the organization of more Ranger companies to fight the criminal element, and talked of cattle and general matters. At last the governor saw Mark out, apologizing for not being able to offer the same standard of hospitality and sport received when he had visited the OD Connected shortly before taking office.

At lunch Mark met Bragg and a number of the men who had shared his first night in the Bigfoot Saloon. After the meal they went to the rear of the livery barn housing both Mark's and Bragg's horses to pitch horseshoes.

The game had been going for some time when an interruption came. Riding tired horses, the sheriff's posse came from off the range. At the lead rode Sheriff Jules Murat, a tall, slim, handsome man who wore range clothes, yet managed to give the appearance of being dressed in some fancy European Hussar's uniform and that he should wear a cavalry saber instead of the two matched Army Colts holstered at his sides. A successful rancher, he had accepted the post of county sheriff—soon to be followed by appointment to captain of a Texas Rangers company—to do a job of work and not as an office-filler mainly concerned with politics or lining his pockets. One of Mark's chief concerns for Belle's safety had been the knowledge that Jules Murat would be hunting for her.

Urging his mount at a faster pace, Murat cut ahead of the rest of the posse and drew rein before the horseshoe pitchers. His eyes went straight to Mark and Bragg, worry in them as he started to speak.

"Mark, Tule, there's bad trouble."

Looking past Murat, Mark and Bragg saw a tarp-wrapped figure draped across the back of a harness horse. Before Mark could start to think that Belle had been shot and told of their part in her escape, Bragg let out a low curse and headed toward the posse. Then Mark noticed that three more members of the sheriff's party led harness horses, although without the sinister load of the first. Next Mark realized that the shape wrapped in a tarpaulin sheet would be too big for Belle. Suddenly, with shocking impact, he understood what made Bragg act in such a manner. Murat dropped from his saddle at Mark's side.

"Is it———?" Mark began.

"It's Sailor Sam," agreed the sheriff quietly.

"An accident?"

"No, Mark," Murat replied.

"Then what———?" Mark demanded.

"We'd been out since morning and nary a sign of whoever robbed Snodgrass could we find. Coming back in we saw where a wagon'd been driven off the trail. It had maybe six riders with it, so we followed the line. Found it in a clearing down close to the Colorado———"

"And?"

"Don't ask me what'd happened. All the gear'd been turned out of the wagon, opened up. There were signs of a helluva fight and Sam'd been shot in the back of the head."

"So you brought his body in," Mark said.

"We'd tired horses under us, Mark," Murat replied. "It'd been afore noon that they shot Sam and left soon after. With a start like that, we needed fresh mounts to catch up."

"Sure you did, Jules," Mark admitted and walked to where Bragg stood cursing in a low, savage voice. "Let's get our rifles and the hosses, Tule."

While the other players seethed with questions they wished to ask Murat, all remained silent as they realized the gravity of the situation. Hearing what Mark said, one of them stepped forward.

"Do you need any help, *amigo*?" he asked and it was a genuine offer, not made out of a morbid desire to take part in a manhunt.

"No thanks," Mark gritted. "Tule and me'll tend to all that needs doing."

"Let me go get a fresh horse and I'll ride with you," Murat put in.

Without any hestitation Mark gave his agreement. Murat might be sheriff of the county which housed the state's capital, but he was also a mighty efficient, practical peace officer. Shrewd, capable, honest, he fought crime hard and, where necessary, trod on toes without a thought of their owner's social standing. Such a man would do to ride the river with and be of the greatest help in the grim work ahead of them.

"Do you have anybody who can read sign, Jules?" Mark asked.

"Tejas Tom there," the sheriff replied, indicating a tall young Indian wearing a town suit, collarless shirt and derby hat. "Don't let his duds fool you, he'd run the Ysabel Kid a close second in reading sign."

"We'll see to Sam for you, Mark," one of the horseshoe pitchers promised. "You go fetch what you'll need; I reckon we can saddle your hosses."

"Thanks," Mark replied. "I'll pay for the burying, so see he gets the best."

Half an hour later Mark rode out of Austin with Bragg, Murat and Tejas Tom, the last two on fresh mounts. During the ride, Murat went into greater detail of what they saw and deduced from the Indian's reading of the sign.

"I'd say those fellers laid for him, hiding just off the trail," Murat told Mark and Bragg. "Made him drive down there where they couldn't be seen. Then it looked like he lit into them."

"Plenty big fight," confirmed the Indian. "That feller put two-three down at least afore they shoot him."

That figured to anybody who knew the fistfighting ability of Sailor Sam. The knowledge that his old tutor went down fighting made Mark feel a little better, although it did nothing to lessen his determination that Sam's killers would pay.

Two miles out of town Murat brought his horse to a halt and pointed to a clump of scrub oak trees close by it. "This's where it happened. They hid up in the trees and rode out peaceable like. Then they took him off toward the river."

Following the direction Murat indicated, Mark saw the tracks left by Sailor Sam's killers. While he did not put himself in the same category as the Ysabel Kid when it came to reading sign, Mark could tell that the men had ridden from their cover at a leisurely pace. Most likely Sailor Sam took them for a bunch of cowhands heading into Austin and looking to pass the time of day with him. By the time he realized the danger, it was too late to escape. So he behaved sensibly, going along with the gun-backed orders while watching for a chance to turn the tables on his captors. At the other side of the trail he saw where the wagon left, escorted by the cook's killers. Starting his horse moving, Mark followed the tracks.

None of the party spoke as they rode through the wooded country in the direction of the Colorado

River. Then at the foot of the slope, well-hidden from the trail, they came into sight of the wagon. Apart from unhitching the team and taking the cook's body along, nothing had been moved. Boxes and barrels lay on the ground, their tops opened and a few contents scattered.

At Murat's suggestion they left the horses well clear of the wagon and went forward on foot. Tejas Tom took the lead and as he drew near the foot of the slope began to describe the men who made the different sign.

"One was big feller, plenty hefty, ride bay mare. Two of 'em tall, lean, got dun and blue roan. 'Nother middle height, heavy with it, ride bay man-hoss. Other two maybe five foot ten, one lean, other heavy, got a black and iron grey hoss."

Having seen the Ysabel Kid in action, Mark knew just how accurate a well-trained visual tracker could be. He did not doubt that when they finally caught up to the gang, the descriptions would prove correct. Going on, Tejas told how Sailor Sam fought and finally went down, shot by the tallest of the slim men. The Indian took Mark and Bragg to where a small rock rose from the springy grass. There they saw the marks made by a man falling down hard, but the Indian showed them something more important.

"See um?" he asked, pointing to a black mark on the side of the rock. "Him shoot from ground after him knocked down."

Igniting black powder threw out an awesome muzzle-blast as Mark well knew, but only in a forward direction. Which meant that the man must have held his gun barely out of the holster to shoot. Then Mark remembered the Wycliffe clan. The men he met in the Bigfoot Saloon fitted the description of part of the gang. More than that, Billy Wycliffe carried his gun in a swivel holster and did not need to draw the weapon to shoot. Fired from the leather, his Colt's barrel would have been low and close enough to leave the powder burns on the rock.

At which point the Indian dropped another bombshell. "Was girl with wagon."

For a moment the words did not sink into Mark's furiously thinking head. Then he stared from Tejas to Bragg and said, "A girl?"

"Not from the herd, that's for sure," Bragg stated.

"Sign show she jump off box and run. Feller go after her and drag her back. They take her with 'em when the go."

"Sam must've picked her up on the way in," Murat guessed. "Maybe from one of them nester spreads down that ways."

"I reckon I know who killed Sam," Mark said quietly.

"Who?" asked the sheriff.

"Billy Wycliffe."

"Why him?"

"We had a run-in with 'em last night," Mark explained. "Billy was wearing his gun in a half-breed holster."

Having seen the powder blackening on the rock, Murat knew what Mark meant. However he did not take the other's suggestion at blind face value.

"And you figure they jumped Sam to get even?" he asked.

"No," admitted Mark. "I don't reckon they'd go a round-about way like that to get even with anybody."

"Weren't but four of 'em we saw," Bragg reminded Mark.

"Way the fellers at the Bigfoot talked, there're plenty more," Mark replied.

"That's for sure," Murat agreed. "Only you can't be sure it was them, Mark."

"Everything points that way," Mark replied, his

big hands working in the unspoken, deadly rage which filled him. "We'll know for sure when we find them."

"Likely," answered the sheriff.

"It's a heap more than likely!" Mark snapped. "Sam fought back. That means all of them are carrying marks he gave them."

"Let's go get 'em!" growled Bragg.

"We haven't more than a couple of hours afore dark," objected Murat.

"We'll have a start for morning," Mark put in. "Maybe you'd best leave it to Tule and me, Jules."

"To run them down and nail their hides to the wall?"

"Something like that."

"Is that the way Hondo and Dusty Fog taught you to handle the law?"

"Damn it to hell, Jules!" Mark snapped. "You knew Sailor Sam. He was a good-hearted cuss who never did harm to anybody who wasn't asking for it. He worked for pappy near as long as Tule here———"

"Which shouldn't stop you thinking and acting right," Murat said quietly. "Sailor Sam was your friend, Mark. Only if you start thinking on that instead of on proving who killed him, you could make a mistake."

"Maybe," Mark replied.

"There's no maybe about it and you know it!" Murat snapped. "Sure everything points to the Wycliffe bunch. Only that's a mighty small description Tejas gave us and it could fit plenty of men. I can tell you three fellers in Austin alone who use a half-breed holster, two of them would fit the description of the one who shot Sam if it comes to that."

"You figure one of them two did it?" growled Bragg.

"Nope. One of 'em's a Wells Fargo messenger and

the other works for me as a deputy. I just mentioned them to show you that it could be somebody else," Murat replied. "Not that I reckon the Wycliffes wouldn't put something like this—— But they'd want a reason for doing it."

"Maybe figured to rob Sam," Bragg guessed. "Figured he'd have money to pay for whatever supplies he bought in town."

"Not if it's the Wycliffes," Murat answered. "I wouldn't put robbing a blind man's begging-cup past the young'uns, but Churn's not that cheap. So if he was along, they came after more than the chance of picking up a few hundred dollars. And I went through Sam's pockets; whoever killed him hadn't."

Which ruled out robbery as the motive for the killing. In such a secluded spot, a well-armed gang meaning to steal would not be deterred by having murdered their victim. With robbery apparently ruled out, the question of motive rose once more. It seemed unlikely that the Wycliffes would take their revenge on Sailor Sam, or even that they knew his connection with Mark and Bragg.

"Who's on the trail behind you, Tule?" Mark asked.

"Nobody that we know of."

Occasionally the trail crew following another herd would take steps to slow it down and pass it so as to reach the railhead market first. So every trail boss kept a wary eye on his rear, ready to counter such moves. While killing the cook would have at least nuisance value, Mark doubted if that had been the reason for Sam's murder. Yet it was a possibility, slim maybe, but Mark knew one could not afford to overlook the most slender chance. Murder, very sensibly, carried the death penalty, so a man like Mark Counter knew better than make the mistake of picking the wrong suspect when hunting for a killer.

Murat's warning had worked. With the first flush

of his anger worn off, Mark remembered the training
he received in peace officer work from two of the
most enlightened lawmen in Texas. Although grief
nagged at him, the blond giant forced himself to face
the issue with an open mind. While almost certain
that the Wycliffe clan were behind Sailor Sam's
death, he was prepared to search for other possibilities.

"Let's make a start," he said. "We'll see which
direction they're headed if nothing more."

Satisfied that they could learn no more at the scene
of the crime, Murat gave his agreement to Mark's
suggestion and told Tejas to cut for sign. Quickly the
Indian collected his horse and led the way along the
tracks left by the departing killers. From the leisurely
way the tracks had been made, fear of discovery did
not cause them to leave before looting their victim.
Nor did they go far. Swinging off through the trees,
the tracks halted in cover near the trial. Once again
the horses had been left tied to trees or bushes—it
had been hair rubbed from their coats along with
traces of urine which told the Indian each horse's
color and the fact that one was a mare—while their
riders went on foot to watch the trail.

"Stopped here for a spell," Tejas told the others.
"Maybe hour."

"Looks like they were fixing to grab off and rob
anybody who come along," Bragg growled.

"Or they waited for somebody special," Mark
went on. "Maybe they weren't after Sam at all."

"Whoever it was, they didn't find him," Murat
stated. "They fetched their horses and rode off."

"Go up that way," Tejas said, pointing.

"There's a nester's place maybe two miles along
the trail," Murat commented. "Let's go ask if he's
seen anybody go by."

"He should notice six men and a gal passing,"
Mark said as they started to ride in the direction in-

dicated by Tejas Tom. "If they've still got the gal along."

"They took her," the Indian replied. "Leave her fastened to a tree while wait at side of trail. Then come back for her and hosses."

While riding along, Tejas Tom had the others help him keep watch for sign of the other party leaving the trail. However there were several places at which Sailor Sam's killers could have swung off without leaving any tracks, due to the nature of the ground. Certainly they did not take their horses off at any point where sign would show.

The nester showed some surprise at seeing the sheriff's party ride up to his cabin. However Murat possessed a reputation for fair dealing and was made welcome. Accepting the offer of a cup of coffee, the men dismounted and entered the small cabin. Mark and the others sat around the table while several children hovered in the background and stared wide-eyed at them. When asked if he had seen Sailor Sam's wagon go by, the nester nodded.

"Sure did. He stopped here and had a cup of java, seemed a right friendly sort of a jasper and talked real pleasant."

"Not any more," Bragg put in bluntly. "He's dead."

"The hell you say! And the gal that was with him?"

"They took the gal along with them," Mark told the man.

"I'm not at all surprised!" snorted the woman of the house. "She looked———"

"Hush now, Martha!" the nester said.

"You knew her, ma'am?" asked Murat.

"No. She's not from these parts, I'd swear. Looked like some fancy woman, headed for Austin to work in a saloon."

"She didn't dress like one," objected the nester.

"Or like a decent woman, in her shirt and pants, or with all that paint and powder on her face!" his wife answered.

"She didn't come back this way with maybe six fellers on horses then?" Murat inquired.

"Nope. I've been outside here working all afternoon and nobody come by," the nester replied.

Studying the man, Mark felt sure that he spoke the truth and had not been paid by Sam's killers to remain silent. Which meant that the gang must have left the trail at one of the points where their tracks did not show. Only an extensive search, or some luck, would find the tracks where they left the hard ground. Mark knew that making it at such a late hour of the day would be futile.

"Do you get many wagons coming by here?" he asked, thinking of the gang's actions after leaving Sam's body.

"Some, mostly neighbors or cooks from trail herds going through," the nester replied.

"Don't forget that trader who comes through maybe once a month," his wife put in. "It's near on time he was coming by."

"Trade, ma'am?" Mark repeated.

"Hell yes!" ejaculated the nester. "Him. Why sure. Say, he's a feller with a beard and used a four-hoss wagon just like that the cook this morning drove."

CHAPTER SEVEN

More Visitors for Mr. Counter

THE nester's comment brought Mark and Murat's eyes to him, then they looked at each other. Both saw the implications of the man's words. An entirely new field of conjecture opened for them.

"Do you know him, this trader, Jules?"

"I can't say I do, Mark. They come and go. Unless they break the law, or I had dealings with them before I took on this sheriff's chore, I wouldn't likely get to know any trader."

"But he looked something like Sam," Mark said. "Maybe not much alike, but enough for those jaspers to've made a mistake. They stopped Sam and made him drive off the trail——— Why'd they do that?"

"So they could rob him without being seen," Bragg suggested. "Most folks in Texas take a mighty poor view of robbing going on in plain daylight."

"Then why take him down there and start searching?" asked Mark "Why didn't they just up and drive off with the whole wagonload."

"Could be they wanted to know something from the feller they thought Sam to be," guessed Murat. "Took him down by the river to start asking. Only Sam jumped them and got hisself shot before they had chance to start."

"That fits," Mark agreed. "When he'd been shot,

73

they searched the wagon and must've guessed they'd picked the wrong man. So they went back to the trail and waited again."

"Then maybe saw my posse in the distance and lit out," Murat finished. "We came on to the trail between where they watched the first and second times, so we missed finding the place where they waited for the feller they wanted."

"As soon as the burying's done tomorrow, we'll start looking," Mark said.

"I'll have Tejas out at dawn to see what he can find," Murat promised.

"How about Banker Snodgrass?" asked Mark.

"How about him?" countered the sheriff.

"He'll expect you to be hunting for whoever robbed him."

"Likely. Only I rate murder and the abduction of a girl a whole heap more pressing and serious than the theft of money. Besides, he's got all that high-priced Pinkerton help to do his hunting."

"You couldn't be a mite jealous, now could you, Jules?" Mark grinned.

"Nope," Murat answered with a smile twisting at his lips. "But I figure any man who hires private law shouldn't expect the local peace officers to bust a gut helping him when he gets robbed. Say, I hear that you had a mishap with one of the Pink-eyes, Mark."

'It was all their fool fault!'' Bragg snorted.

"So I heard," Murat said complacently. "Only, was I you, I'd watch them, Mark. They won't forget what you did to their man."

"I'll watch," Mark promised. "Let's get moving, shall we?"

"Sure," agreed Murat. "Thanks for the java, ma'am."

While riding back in the direction of Austin, Mark turned to the sheriff. "I wonder if they've still got the gal with them, Jules?"

"Likely. They'll not kill her unless they have to."

"That's for sure," Mark admitted.

Killing a woman, even one not regarded as socially acceptable, ranked among the most heinous crimes out West. Any man who did so could expect to be hunted down without mercy. Every hand would be against him; even other outlaws declined to accept a woman-killer in their midst. So Sailor Sam's killers would keep the girl alive as long as possible.

"If she is a saloon gal, they might talk her round to forgetting what she's seen," Murat remarked.

"And she'll make a dandy hostage should the law start crowding them, or get them pinned down someplace," Mark went on. "Should we catch up to them, we'll have to handle things careful to keep her alive."

"What happens if we can't find their tracks?" Bragg demanded.

"I'll telegraph every town and stage relay station in the area, ask them to watch for half-a-dozen riders and a girl, some of the fellers looking like they've been in a fistfight," Murat replied.

"And if nothing comes of it?" insisted the foreman.

"I'll get word to Dusty and the Kid," Mark stated. "Then we'll drift up Sam Saba way and look in on the Wycliffes."

"You're still set on it being them, Mark?" asked the sheriff.

"Sure enough, Jules," Mark answered. "Only I figure there's more chance of me learning something happen I take a couple of friends along to watch my back when I start asking."

On their return to town, Mark and Bragg put up their horses at the livery barn. Its owner, an old and trusted friend, complained with salty bitterness at their lack of success and heaped curses on the heads of Sam's killers. Then he offered to hold the two men's rifles with the saddles that night ready for use in the morning. After attending to their mounts and locking the rifles away, the owner pointed to a bunch of lathered horses which his help cleaned up after hard use.

"Damned Pink-eye sneaks!" he grunted with all the contempt of a Texan for men who neglected their horses. "They've been out all day trying to find whoever robbed Snodgrass and come back in all pot-boiling mad 'cause they couldn't pick up a track."

"It won't do them city jaspers any harm to get out and breathe good Texas air," Bragg grinned.

"Sure won't," agreed the owner. "Only this bunch aren't appreciating it."

"They can allus go back where they come from," the foreman commented.

"Say, Mark," the owner said. "You killed a bounty hunter called Framant last year, didn't you?"

"I figured it was the best thing to do at the time," Mark answered, "seeing how he was fixing to shoot me."

"That Burbage jasper was telling three of the Pink-eyes about it just afore they left here. Sounded real interested."

"He maybe reckons Mark might've got the taste for gunning bounty hunters," suggested Bragg dryly.

"Could be," cackled the old owner.

"Now they know about you and Framant," Bragg said as he and Mark walked out of the barn.

"Word about that kind of thing gets around," Mark answered.

"Reckon they can tie you in with Belle from it?"

"I don't know. The marshal up to Elkhorn never let on to anybody that she was mixed in the game. Only me, him, Belle and Calamity Jane knew the truth."

"Calamity had no cause to like Belle, from what I heard," Bragg commented. "They had one helluva fight, way you told it."

The previous night Mark had told Bragg about the happenings in Elkhorn when he first met both Belle Starr and Calamity Jane. Knowing he could rely on the foreman's discretion, Mark gave almost the full details of the affair.

"They laid into each other until they both got tuckered out," Mark admitted with a grin. "But after it Calam helped me smuggle Belle out of town and risked getting shot to save her. Nope, Calam wouldn't talk out of turn."

"I know I'd never heard who the other gal was, 'cepting a blackjack dealer in a saloon," Bragg said. "But if they should know you stopped Framant laying hands on her, they could get all suspicious and fancy notions about you jumping that yahoo in the hotel."

"We'll just have to worry about that when it comes," Mark stated. "Let's go down to the sheriff's office and see if Jules knows anything."

At the office they waited until Murat returned from sending out telegraph messages to peace officers in the surrounding towns, although both realized that no answer could be expected until much later. When Murat came in, he told them what he had done so far and discussed their line of action for the following day. With that attended to, Mark and Bragg left. They visited the undertaker's shop to which Sailor Sam's body had been taken and satisfied themselves that everything would be as the cook wanted in the matter of the burial.

"We'll have to let pappy know about Sam," Mark said as they left the building. "You wouldn't go tell him, I reckon."

"You reckon right!" snorted Bragg. "Write him about it and we'll get some cowhand to take the letter out."

"Come on then, we'll do it at the hotel," Mark said. "After we've got it off, we'll go down to see

Jules in case he's heard anything. They do say he plays a mean game of checkers.''

"That'll be something," sniffed Bragg.

On their arrival at the Houston Hotel, the reception clerk held out a message form. "This just came for you, Mr. Counter."

"Its from Ole Devil," Mark told Bragg after reading the message. "He says Dusty won't need help and for me to come on home."

"What'll you do?" asked the foreman.

"Telegraph to tell him what's happened and say I'm going after Sam's killer," Mark replied.

"Reckon he'll object?"

"Nope. He'll likely send Dusty and the Kid out to help me. Let's get that letter to pappy written."

Taking his key from the clerk, Mark led the way upstairs and to his room. After unlocking the door, he shoved it open and let Bragg go in first. As the foreman started to enter, removing his hat, an arm holding a wicked leather-wrapped billy lashed at his head from inside the room. No man grew up in the wild frontier country of Texas without developing fast reflexes. Hearing the faint hissing sound, Bragg jerked his hat back on to his head so that the billy struck its crown. While that broke the full force of the blow, it still arrived with enough power to drop him unconscious to the floor.

Like a flash Mark lunged forward, hands reaching for the arm which struck down his friend. Even as his fingers closed on their objective, Mark heard a sound from the other side of the door and saw it start to swing close. The lamp had been lit and turned down to a faint glow. By its light he saw a tall man in range clothing by the wardrobe and a second, a slightly shorter dude, at the window.

All that registered in his mind as he laid hold of the arm of Bragg's attacker. Before any of the men in the room realized just how wrong their plan had gone,

Mark gave a swinging heave at the trapped arm. A startled, agony-filled yelp rose as the billy slipped from limp fingers. Then Quigg, the Pinkerton agent, swung into sight. His feet struck against Bragg's body and he tripped to crash his head into the door.

Bracing himself, Mark kicked hard at the door, slamming it back into the man behind it and hearing a pain-filled curse in a Western voice. Then he heaved Quigg back again, twisting the man around to slam into the wall. As Quigg struck, Mark released him and he collapsed forward limply.

Bounding over Bragg's body, Mark saw the other two men rushing at him. He clenched his fists and whipped them both up and out in backhand swings that drove hard knuckles into his attackers' faces. Each man shot away, spun around by the force of the blows.

Blood running from his nose, Burbage sprang from behind the door. Mark heard him coming and turned. Going under the blow Burbage lashed at him, Mark hit the man in the stomach. Before he could follow up his advantage, the man in range clothes reached him. Mark felt the other's fist catch him at the side of the face and staggered. Driven sideways by the force of the blow, Mark brought himself to a halt. His attacker sprang after him and the second dude rushed forward holding a billy like Quigg used. Out shot Mark's hands, grabbing the Westerner by the shirt front. Then Mark pivoted around, swinging the man. Too late the dude saw what Mark intended. Already the billy rose and hissed through the air in a blow aimed at Mark's head, but the blond giant moved backward. With a dull thud, the billy landed on the Western man's head and the force of his being turned had caused his hat to fly off. So he lacked the protection Bragg's Stetson afforded when Quigg made the treacherous attack.

Feeling the man he held go limp, Mark hurled him

at the billy-armed dude. Struck by the flying body, the dude reeled backward. He and the unconscious Westerner went down with a crash by the wardrobe. The force of their arrival caused its door to commence opening. Then, in an inexplicable manner, the door reversed direction. It slid back until amost closed, remaining still maybe an inch from its shut position.

Burbage caught Mark's arm, turned him and hit him in the face. Across whipped the man's other fist, snapping Mark's head the other way. Closing in, Burbage felt hands like steel traps clamp on his vest. To his amazement he felt himself lifted and hurled over Bragg's body through the door. Landing on his feet, Burbage could not prevent himself continuing backward and his progress was halted by colliding with the door of the room facing Mark's.

Spluttering curses, the dude rolled his limp companion from him and sat up. His billy lay halfway across the room where he dropped it when struck by his companion's body, but he made no attempt to reach it. Instead he drew the Smith & Wesson No. 2 revolver from its holster. A puny weapon to most range-dwellers' way of thinking, the .32 bullet would still kill or wound at close range, given the chance. As Mark had his back to the other man, it seemed that the chance was being presented. Up lifted the revolver, for the man did not intend to miss if he could help it. So engrossed was he in taking aim that he did not see the wardrobe door open, or notice the arm which came from inside. Down drove the arm, clothed in a dark shirt sleeve and hand gripping around the frame of what at first sight looked like a Navy Colt. The butt of the weapon landed with some force on top of the dude's head and he collapsed as if he had been boned, the Smith & Wesson dropping unfired at his side. Instantly the arm disappeared into the wardrobe and the door closed completely.

Mark heard the sound behind him, so turned ready to deal with whatever fresh menace might arise. Before he faced into the room, the wardrobe door had shut and he stared wonderingly at the sprawled out shape of the dude. Time to think over what caused the dude's condition was not granted to the blond giant. Three of his attackers might be rendered *hors de combat*—although he could not think how one of them came to be so—yet a fourth and maybe the most dangerous remained active. Just how active Mark rapidly discovered.

After hitting the door facing Mark's room, Burbage bounced forward a step before digging in his heels and bringing himself to a halt. While determined to take revenge for his rough treatment at the blond giant's hands, Burbage had no desire to continue fighting with fists. Twice he had received samples of Mark's great strength and seen enough to warn him that further fistfighting was out. Seeing the big blond's back toward him, Burbage grabbed for his gun. The door into which he had collided opened and an indignant-looking man glared out. Seeing Burbage reaching for a gun, taken with the sight of Bragg sprawled in the doorway opposite, the man's indignation became rapidly tinted with caution. His angry demand to be told what the hell somebody thought by damned nigh knocking the door off its hinges died with barely four words said. Retreating hurriedly, he slammed the door closed and twisted himself with some rapidity around until he stood with the wall and not the door's flimsy paneling between himself and any stray flying bullets.

Hearing the sound behind him, Burbage tried to do two things at once. The Houston catered for a good class of customer, and there was a possibility that whoever opened the door might be Mark Counter's friend, in which case Burbage knew a warning would be given, at least, or possibly a bullet driven into him

to stop his attempt on the blond giant's life. No
Texas jury would convict a man who used a gun to
prevent somebody shooting another in the back. So
Burbage looked over his shoulder, but did not
prevent his hand drawing the gun. Such were the
trained reflexes a man like Burbage possessed that he
completed his draw and fired while still looking
away. A man shooting for pleasure or practice might
have felt highly satisfied by the result, for the bullet
sent Mark's hat spinning from his head and punc-
tured a hole in the top of its crown. Not bad shooting
under the circumstances—if Burbage shot for
pleasure or practice.

Only he did not. His bullet had been intended to
cripple Mark and, in missing, achieved nothing more
than to warn him of his danger. As the big blond
whirled around, his right hand dropped down to and
drew the offside Colt. Already angry at the
treacherous attack, Mark did not hesitate in his actions. He did not know that Burbage merely meant to
wound him, nor would the knowledge have made
him feel any more inclined to leniency. All he knew
was that a man tried to shoot him and stood holding
a revolver capable of being used for another attempt.
So Mark countered the threat as fast and completely
as he could manage.

Flame tore from the barrel of Mark's Colt. Like
Burbage, he shot from waist high and by instinctive
alignment. Only he looked toward his target and had
nothing to distract his attention. The .44 bullet drove
into Burbage's shoulder, spinning him around and
causing him to drop his gun. Striking the wall instead
of the door, he slid down to the floor. Pain tore
through him and his right arm felt numb, refusing to
obey the dictates of his mind. Through the haze that
misted his eyes he saw the revolver and reached
toward it with his left hand.

After shooting, Mark lunged through the door. He

cocked the long-barreled Colt on its recoil, ready to shoot again. Nor would he have hesitated to do so if the man showed any sign of fight. Stepping across the passage, Mark kicked the revolver from Burbage's reach. Foiled in his attempt, the man gave a low moan and went limp, flopping forward on to his face.

Voices raised in the lobby and feet thudded to, then up the stairs. Doors along the passage opened, people looking out cautiously. Seeing that there did not appear to be any chance of further shooting, the guests left their rooms. Most of them knew Mark and put the shooting down to his having disturbed a thief in his room or about to enter it.

Ignoring the guests who converged on him and the clerk appearing at the head of the stairs. Mark returned to Bragg's side. Holstering his Colt, Mark knelt by the foreman. An expression of relief came to the blond giant's face as he saw Bragg start to force himself up. A glance into his room told Mark that there would be no further trouble from that direction. Then he looked at Bragg who had reached hands and knees, staying there while shaking his head to clear it.

"Whooee!" Bragg groaned as Mark helped him to rise. "What happened? Who in hell done it to me?"

"What's happening here?" demanded the clerk, forcing his way through the guests and speaking before Mark could answer Bragg's question.

"How'd you feel, Tule!" Mark asked.

"Lousy. What happened?"

"The Pink-eyes jumped us."

Despite being dazed by the blow and dizzy from it, Bragg did not make any incautious or incriminating statement. Putting his shoulder against the door jamb, he looked first at Burbage and then into the room.

"Did I get any of 'em?" he asked.

"None, you just lay down and slept through it all," Mark replied and turned to glare at the desk clerk. "Just what kind of a place do you reckon to run? Last night I see a feller in a gal's room and figure he's robbing it. Now I come here and get jumped by a bunch of yahoos."

Figuring that the best defense was a good strong attack, Mark launched it immediately. He did not know how much the Pinkerton agents told the desk clerk, or what excuse they made to obtain entrance to his room, but decided to arouse doubts in the man's mind before any of his assailants could contradict it.

Surprise showed on the clerk's face as he stared first at Burbage and then into the room. "I assure you, Mr. Counter, that I had no idea they were even in the hotel!" he squeaked with such sincerity that Mark believed him.

Before he could say any more, Mark saw the bellhop and two deputy marshals appear at the head of the stairs. Thrusting through the crowd, the peace officers holstered the revolvers they drew when climbing the stairs.

"Howdy, Mark," said the taller of the pair. "What happened?"

"This bunch jumped me," Mark replied.

"Hey!" yipped the second deputy. "That's Burbage, he's been working with them Pinkerton sneaks——"

"You'll find three more in the room there," Mark told him.

"You shoot 'em too?"

"We only heard one shot, Buck," the taller deputy reminded.

"There were two fired," Mark said. "That feller put a hole in my hat."

"Tried to shoot this gent in the back, too," put in the man from the room opposite and whose actions saved Mark from injury.

"What set 'em on to you, Mark?" asked the taller deputy.

"I rough-handled one of them last night———"

"So I heard. Looks like they figured to jump you and get even. They lay for you in your room?"

"Sure," Mark agreed. "Only being a gentleman I let my guest walk in first."

"Gentleman nothing!" snorted Bragg, holding his hat in one hand while he delicately ran a fingertip across his skull. "I reckon he knowed they was there and sent me in first to get whomped on the head."

"You'd maybe best make sure they didn't steal anything, Mark," the taller deputy suggested. "We'll tend to their needings."

Entering the room, the two deputies hauled the Westerner and dude toward the door. While they did so, Mark crossed to the wardrobe. He doubted if the Pinkerton men would have searched his property, but noticed that the wardrobe key was no longer in the lock. Yet it had been when he left the room. So he walked to the door and tugged at its handle.

Fortunately the deputies had their backs to him and none of the people in the passage could see past his powerful frame. The wardrobe's door began to open and Mark became aware that it held something not there when he last looked inside. Only with an effort did he prevent an exclamation of surprise from slipping out and he closed the door before the deputies could learn what lay behind it.

"They didn't take a thing," he said and hoped that his voice sounded natural.

CHAPTER EIGHT

A Debt Repaid

THE taller of the deputies proved to be a man of action. A doctor staying at the hotel had already attended to the wounded Burbage. After dispersing the remainder of the crowd, the deputy gave thought to disposing of the rest of Mark's attackers. He looked at the groaning men, then turned to the big blond.

"Do you want for me to haul them down to the pokey, Mark?"

"You'd best until their boss allows that they'll steer clear of me," Mark replied. "The next time I might not go so easy on them."

"I'll see he gets to know," the deputy promised, walking to where Quigg sat by the door. "All right, *hombre*, on your feet."

Realizing the futility of argument, Quigg rose and helped the other dude lift the still unconscious Westerner. Then the two deputies escorted the men from the room. Mark followed them and prepared to defend his position to the desk clerk.

"I can't tell you how sorry I am, Mr. Counter," the man said before Mark could start. "But I didn't know they had come into the hotel, or were in your room."

"It's not your fault," Mark replied. "I'm sorry it happened."

Leaving the removal of Burbage and the other men to the deputies, Mark entered his room. After doing what he could to save Burbage's life, the doctor went to check whether any of the others suffered damage. With the passage clear, Mark returned to his room. Watched by a surprised-looking Bragg, he locked the door and then drew the curtains before turning up the lamp.

"What the————?" Bragg began.

"You can come out now," Mark said in the direction of the wardrobe.

Bragg had taken a seat on the edge of the bed, but he bounced to his feet as if the cover was red hot. With bugged-out eyes he stared at the wardrobe door, which opened apparently of its own volition.

At another time Mark might have found the sight of Bragg's show of emotion to be amusing. Under normal conditions he would have been pleased to see a beautiful young woman—even if she also were an outlaw—stepping from his wardrobe. Neither sight particularly attracted him at that moment.

Dressed in the same clothing she wore when they last saw her, Belle walked across the room. She read disapproval on Mark's face and hurried to explain her conduct.

"I had to come back, Mark. I know who killed Sailor Sam—and why."

"So that's why you risked your fool neck," Mark growled.

"Why else?" smiled the girl. "You took a big chance for me, both here and in Elkhorn."

"It was a pleasure both times," Mark assured her. "Only I don't————"

A knock at the door chopped his words off. Swiftly Belle darted across the room and disappeared into the wardrobe, closing the door behind her. Bragg resumed his seat and adopted an attitude of studious innocence. Walking to the door, Mark unlocked and opened it. He found the doctor and desk clerk standing outside.

"Your friend was hurt, Mr. Counter," said the latter. "So I asked the doctor if he would come up and examine him—at the hotel's expense of course."

For a moment Mark hesitated, then decided that having witnesses to the fact that apparently only he and Bragg were in the room might be advantageous. So he thanked the clerk for showing such consideration and allowed the doctor to enter. Despite being eager to hear what Belle had to say about the murder of Sailor Sam, Mark forced himself to stand and wait while the examination of Bragg's head took place. After what seemed a long time, although it was not, the doctor straightened up and grinned.

"You'll do," he told Bragg. "It raised one hell of a knob, but hasn't done any damage or broken the skin. Those leather-wrapped billies don't cut as a rule."

"How about the feller I shot?" asked Mark.

"He'll live, but won't be getting around for a spell. Should think himself lucky for all that. I don't reckon you picked that particular spot to hit him."

"That's for sure," Mark admitted and glanced at his bullet-holed Stetson. "I just pulled and cut loose to stop him improving his aim. Thanks, doctor. If this worthless ole goat————"

"He means me," Bragg put in.

"Who else?" demanded Mark. "If this worthless ole goat lives————"

"You mean you reckon you can kill a cowhand by whomping him on the head?" grinned the doctor. "That's not what he works with. I wonder how much the hotel'll go for?"

After the doctor left, Belle came once more from the wardrobe. She walked to the bed and sat on its edge, crossing one shapely, trouser-clad leg over the other and looking at the expectant faces of the men.

"I got clear of the hotel with no trouble and went to hide out with friends in town," she explained. "Figuring on staying with them until things quietened down a mite. Only when I hard about Sam, I decided to help you.''

''How?'' asked Mark.

''You remember that I said somebody had sold me to the Pink-eyes?''

''Sure.''

''And that I thought I knew who it might be?''

''Yep,'' agreed Mark.

''Well, I had my friends get the feller and fetch him to see me. They had masks on and blindfolded him so that he doesn't know where he is. I questioned him about the killing————''

''Who is he?'' growled Bragg.

''That's not why I came here,'' the girl answered. ''He bought his life by telling me everything about Sailor Sam—and it was plenty.''

''Such as?'' asked Mark.

''Firstly, Sam was killed by mistake; which makes it a damned sight worse. Churn Wycliffe's bunch were waiting for a trader who ought to have come into town along that trail. Their descriptions tallied, so Wycliffe thought Sam was the man he wanted.''

''Was this feller there when it happened?'' demanded Bragg.

''No. He told me about the Wycliffes waiting for the wagon and described the driver. So I guessed what had happened.''

''It was Billy Wycliffe who shot Sam,'' Mark told Belle. ''We read that from the sign out there. Where are they now?''

''I don't know, nor does the man who told me about it,'' Belle admitted. ''But I may be able to help you find them. You know Runcorne of the Lone Rider Saloon?''

''Not to speak to, but I've heard about him and've seen his place.''

''Well, he's been trading whisky, guns and other stuff to the Kaddo Indians for silver. Not silver money, but mined bars of it. I think it comes from some deserted and lost Spanish diggings the Kaddos found.''

"This feller told you about it?" Mark inquired.

"He told me," Belle agreed. "And he makes most of his living by picking up information. It seems that he sold the news to Wycliffe who planned to learn where the silver came from by forcing the trader to talk."

"So that's why they took Sam off the trail," Mark said. "Only he jumped the whole damned bunch of them and Billy shot him."

"I bet Churn nearly killed Billy for doing it," Belle replied.

"When I get hold of Billy, he'll wish he had," Mark promised. "You wouldn't like to tell me who the man is who told you all this, Belle?"

"No. Like I said, he bought his life with the information."

"I could guess, but I won't," the blond giant drawled, thinking of the meeting between Wycliffe and the pedlar that he witnessed at the Bigfoot Saloon. "Only I don't see why he told you all this."

"Not because he suspects about you and me," Belle assured him. "He wanted to buy his life, figuring I might aim to kill him for selling me out to the Pink-eyes. His idea was that I and my 'gang' went after Wycliffe's bunch, then took the silver from them after they found it."

A faint smile flickered across Belle's face at the thought. Her "gang" had only two other members; an elderly man of somber if commanding, appearance and a mild-natured young feller with considerable skill at opening locked safe doors. Neither of the men who brought the informer to her had been involved in the robbery and Belle had nothing that might by any but the wildest stretch of the imagination be called a gang. However the informer knew nothing of that, believing, like many other people, that Belle commanded a large, well-organized gang willing to carry out her orders.

"Then Wycliffe's likely to be watching the trail," Mark said, guessing at Belle's thoughts.

"Unless he's already met the trader and learned what he needs to know," the girl agreed. "If he has, he'll be headed for the place."

"Your feller didn't say where that'd be?" asked Bragg.

"He swears he doesn't know and I think he's scared enough not to lie," Belle replied. "If he had known, Wycliffe wouldn't've needed to grab off the trader and ask about it."

"That figures," Mark went on. "But I'd like to know where to go in case Wycliffe's already met the feller and learned how to find the silver."

"You could try asking Runcorne," Belle suggested. "He knows."

"Reckon he'd tell us?" asked Bragg.

"If we ask him real polite," Mark answered and looked at the girl. "What do you aim to do about this talkative jasper now, Belle?"

"Turn him clear and steer well clear of him in the future. And, if he's one ounce of good sense, he'll do the same with me."

"You maybe better find some way to tell him to ride a wide circle around me from now on," Mark said. "I'd as soon not see him again, seeing as how he helped get Sam killed."

"I don't think you need worry about that," the girl replied. "And don't look worried. I'm not planning to kill him. But one day somebody will, the way he tries to run with the fox and hunt with the hounds."

Belle wondered how Mark came to tie the pedlar Jacobs in with Wycliffe, for he had not mentioned seeing the men talking in the Bigfoot Saloon. Less than a year later her prediction came true. After selling information to Murat about the leader of a gang of cow thieves, Jacobs made the mistake of falling into the person he sold's hands and paid the penalty.*

"Let's go see Runcorne, Tule," Mark ordered. "What're you going to do, Belle, wait here for me?"

"I think not," she smiled. "Maybe Shafto'll start putting things together when he hears why his men came after you. So I'd better be away from here before he puts a watch on the place."

"It'd likely be best," Mark admitted. "I'll see you around."

"That's for sure," she replied. "I'm sorry about what happened to Sam."

"So'll the Wycliffes be when we catch up to 'em," promised Bragg.

"There's one other thing," the girl said as the men prepared to leave the room. "Runcorne keeps the silver and a stock of trade goods hidden in the wine barrels in his saloon's cellar. The feller told me that and suggested we raided them."

"We'll mind it," Mark said and put his hands on her shoulders. Gently he kissed her and then went on. "You ride careful, Belle honey. Or have you decided to take up that feller's offer?"

"I told him my mammy didn't raise any idiot children."

"She raised a mighty smart one," complimented Bragg.

"Only half-smart, pulling a fool game like this tonight," Mark replied.

"You helped me out twice," she pointed out. "I like to repay my debts."

"Maybe you'd best stay here, Tule," Mark said. "That was a nasty crack you got on your pumpkin head."

"I'm over it now," snorted the foreman. "And anyways, you'll likely need somebody to watch your

---

* Told in *The Cow Thieves*.

back at Runcorne's place.''

''*Loco* as a fool-hen,'' grinned Mark. ''And afore you say it, that figures, working for pappy.''

''It's getting so a feller can't speak around here,'' sniffed Bragg. ''Let's go put some custom Mr. Runcorne's way. It couldn't happen to a nicer son-of-a-bitch from what I've heard about him.''

While walking through the streets toward the Lone Rider Saloon, Mark and Bragg discussed Belle's information. They also thought up a scheme by which they could gain entrance to the saloon's cellar. If Belle's informant spoke the truth, neither man expected Runcorne to permit an inspection of his underground storeroom. However, given one little piece of Texas luck, Mark reckoned they could get into the cellar and learn enough to put its owner in a talkative mood.

Although the Lone Rider was as big as the Bigfoot, it catered to a different class of trade. While the Bigfoot drew most of its custom from the higher income bracket, the Lone Rider attracted men of lesser means. So its furnishing and fittings looked cheaply garish, like a dancehall girl's imitation diamonds. Not that the clientele objected, for the place offered them everything they asked for in the way of entertainment and at a lower rate than the more elegant Bigfoot.

Looking around the room on making his entrance, Mark noticed a number of cowhands present. Any man with Mark's practical experience of workers in the major industry of Texas could read the signs. So he guessed that the three groups of cowhands each consisted of a different ranch's crew. The conversation of the previous night at the Bigfoot made no mention of trouble between the local spreads, something certain to be discussed if it existed. Mark felt his scheme would work. Loyalty to the brand he worked for made a cowhand touchy on the subject. He believed his outfit to be the best and was willing to rear back and prove it should any doubts be raised. If necessary Mark intended to make use of that loyalty as an aid to checking on the truth of Belle Star's story.

In addition to the brawny bouncers hovering at strategic points about the room, the waiters also seemed to be selected for muscular development rather than ability at serving drinks. Such men would be able to prevent even the blond giant from gaining unpermitted entrance to the cellar unless diverted.

Which raised another point: locating the cellar's door. Standing just inside the building, as if waiting for somebody or searching the crowd for friends, Mark and Bragg studied the room. A wide staircase led up to a balcony and the saloon's upper floor. That did not interest either man, for what they wanted was a cellar. In addition to the main entrance, customers could come in through smaller doors at the left or right. Again Mark and Bragg ignored the sight, concentrating on three possibilities, none of which struck them as being attractively situated for their purpose.

The three doors studied by Mark were in the wall behind the big bar. Of the three Mark liked the central one least of all. No matter how well his diversion worked, there would be no chance of getting behind the bar undetected. Not that the other two doors offered much greater chances, being set one at each end of the bar.

Even as Mark watched, the door behind the bar opened and a bartender went in. He left the door open, allowing Mark an uninterrupted view of the room beyond. It seemed to be an ordinary small store, shelves holding bottles around the walls.

"That's not it, unless there's a trapdoor in the floor," Mark told Bragg.

"From the way those two jaspers went through the door at the left of the bar, I'd say that wasn't it either," Bragg answered.

Mark had also noticed a townsman and cowhand

pass through the door Bragg mentioned and concluded that it led to a men's room at the rear of the building. So only one possibility remained. And then Mark remembered that most saloon owners had an office on the premises and mostly on the ground floor.

"Where's the boss?" he asked a passing waiter.

Reluctantly the man came to a halt. He eyed the blond giant, first taking in the expensive clothing. Any idea that Mark might be no more than a rich, soft-living dandy affecting cowhand dress died swiftly. Not only did those well-used matched Colts hang just right but under the costly clothes lay muscles equal, if not superior, to those of any man in the room. So the waiter held down his angry comment about having work to do and no time to answer fool questions.

"You want to see him?" he inquired with what passed for politeness.

"Likely," Mark replied.

"That's his office at the right of the bar. Just go up and knock. If he's in, he'll maybe see you."

"Do you-all have snake fights here, feller?" asked Bragg.

"Huh?" grunted the waiter, scowling at Bragg.

Once again belligerence became tinted with caution. While not as imposing a physical specimen as his companion, Bragg did not strike the waiter as easy meat or even a man to be pushed around. There was a leathery toughness about the foreman which hinted that anybody pushing him would be pushed back, even harder.

"Snake fights, friend, that's having two snakes fighting each other in a pit. They have 'em in plenty places down South."

"Sure do," Mark agreed. "In the cellar of the Casa Moreno at San Antonio." He looked at the waiter. "You hold 'em in your cellar, friend?"

Surprise showed on the waiter's face and he darted

a glance in the direction of the stairs. "Naw. We don't have 'em."

"Let's go someplace where they do then," Mark said to Bragg.

"I'll just have me a drink here first," the foreman replied and the waiter walked away before an order could be given. "What do you reckon, boy?"

Looking toward the stairs, Mark saw a door let into the wall beneath them. He had seen it before, but overlooked it as a possibility. From the waiter's involuntary action, Mark concluded that more than a simple broom closet lay behind the door under the stairs.

"I reckon we've found it," Mark replied. "Go do your part."

While Bragg headed for the bar, Mark walked across the room and halted near the cellar door. He ignored the interested glances of a couple of girls and leaned by the door, apparently waiting for his companion to bring a drink.

Like Mark, Bragg knew cowhands. So the foreman saw his task would be much easier than he expected as he approached the bar. At that hour of the night any cowhand in town could be relied upon to be carrying a fair amount of Old Scalp Lifter and in the state of intoxication where one felt on top of the world and ready to prove it against anybody.

Joining a bunch of the cowhands, Bragg offered to set up drinks. He soon learned they belonged to the Bench M, the finest dod-blasted cow outfit ever sired.

"Well then," Bragg said, lifting his glass. "Here's to the Bench M, the best spread in Texas."

"In the United States!" corrected one of the cowhands.

"In the whole danged wide world!" declared another.

Along the bar, one of a second group of cowhands let out a laugh, staring pointedly at the Bench M crew.

"Sounds like somebody don't believe you," Bragg remarked.

"Don't it though," agreed the spokesman for the Bench M. "Anyways, them Bradded A bunch wouldn't know a good cow outfit if it rode all over 'em."

Thrusting himself from his place at the bar, the Bradded A contingent advanced toward Bragg's party. "What'd you say?" he demanded.

"You heard me, your ears're big enough."

"Well you just take it back right now!"

"Make me!"

Before the bartender could signal to the bouncers, the Bradded A's leader threw a punch at the spokesman for the Bench M. Next minute both parties charged at each other with fists flying. Cursing bouncers and waiters began to converge on the spot. Just as Bragg and Mark anticipated, the employees of the saloon were heartily disliked by most of the customers. So the third group of cowhands pitched in to prevent interference with the fight. In a very short time a full-scale battle began to rage. Screaming girls fled from the room and one of them started to blow on a whistle. The short, blocky shape of Runcorne appeared at his office's door and started to howl curses at the fighters, interspersed with orders that his men most probably could not hear.

Nimbly slipping around the edge of the fight, Bragg joined Mark at the cellar door. Already Mark had tried the door and found it locked, which they both expected. However, everybody else either watched or took part in the fight. Mark had created his diversion. Everything now depended on whether he could force an entrance and gain admittance to the cellar.

"We won't have long," the foreman stated. "You'd best go to it."

CHAPTER NINE

The Secret of the Barrels

WHILE Bragg kept watch on the crowd, Mark swung to face the door. The blond giant measured the distance as he flexed his left knee, raised his right leg and drove its boot at the door. Following the method taught to him by Dusty Fog, Mark crashed his foot into the door just below its lock. He did not try to burst open the door, but to spring the lock. Provided that the door did not also have bolts on its inside, he felt he should be able to do so. As his boot collided with the door, his full weight and power went behind it. Immediately the lock cracked and the door flew inward. While the action took only a few seconds, it could not have been performed in full view of the crowd without attracting attention. Engrossed in the fight, nobody saw Mark make his move.

Stepping through the door, Mark found himself at the head of a flight of stairs. Possibly Runcorne expected the arrival of another consignment of silver. Whatever the reason, lamps lit the stairs and cellar. On the surface everything seemed normal enough. Across from the stairs, a chute ran down from the outside entrance. While Mark knew of the chute, it was used for carrying barrels and other items from the side alley into the cellar, he could not make his entrance by it. On reaching the saloon, he and Bragg looked down the alley and saw a pair of armed men standing guard over the cellar door. That fact gave added credence to Belle's story for it seemed unlikely Runcorne would trouble to hire guards over an ordinary cellar's contents.

Cases of whisky, gin and rum bottles were stacked against the walls along with barrels and kegs of beer. Incongruous, considering the type of clientele the Lone Rider attracted, three huge wine barrels rested on racks by the goods chute. According to Belle's informant, the silver and merchandise to be traded to the Indians ought to be inside those big barrels. With such proof Mark figured he could learn all he needed from the saloonkeeper as the price of his silence. Not that Mark intended to allow the trafficking in whisky and arms to the Indians to continue. A hint in the right place would see Jules Murat starting an investigation that ought to put an end to the evil business.

At the foot of the stairs Mark and Bragg started to walk in the direction of the wine barrels.

"Hey, you there!" yelled a voice from behind them.

Turning, they saw a pair of bouncers at the door. One of the burly men started down the stairs but his companion turned to call something in the direction of the barroom. Although he turned to follow his companions, the other had already reached the foot of the stairs.

"Get set, boy!" ordered Bragg and lunged toward the bouncer.

While tough and capable, Bragg was no fool. He knew that he stood no chance should the bouncer lay hands on him. So he planned his move fast. Stout wooden pillars rose from the cellar to support the floor above. Before the bouncer could lay hands on him, Bragg caught hold of the nearest pillar and used it to swing himself clear of the danger. Nor did he allow the matter to end there. Continuing his swing, he came up at the man's rear. Still using his momentum, Bragg brought up both feet and drove them into the man's back. Taken by surprise, the bouncer went shooting forward to where Mark waited. Around lashed the blond giant's fist in a smooth punch to the side of the bouncer's jaw. The blow caused an involuntary and hurried change of direction. Unable to help himself, he went sprawling across the cellar and crashed into a pile of empty crates.

Bouncing down the stairs, the second man flung himself at Bragg. Before the big hands clamped hold of him, Bragg sidestepped. He snapped up his right foot with all the ease of a French-Creole *savate* fighter, sending the toe of his boot into the bouncer's belly. A croak of agony burst from the man and he doubled over as he blundered by Bragg. Pivoting around, the foreman placed his boot against the other's rump and shoved hard. Shooting forward, the man rushed toward Mark. Down came Mark's hand, catching the bouncer by the scruff of the neck and heaving to send him flying after his companion. Colliding with the wall, the man crumpled and collapsed limply.

"Let's get to those barrels, *pronto*!" Mark suggested.

"Hold it right there!" ordered a voice from the head of the stairs.

Followed by two of his men, Runcorne started down into the cellar. He came with a face showing fury and a gun in his hand. Glancing at Bragg, Mark saw he did not need to pass any warning. The foreman realized the danger just as well as Mark and did not plan to make any wrong moves.

"Howdy," Bragg greeted politely.

"What're you doing in here?" Runcorne demanded.

"Looking for the way out," answered Bragg.

"That door was locked————!"

"Could be we'd heard how good a wine you sell and figured to try some," Mark interrupted.

Emotions flickered across the man's face as he

drew closer. Anger, a hint of fear and some curiosity warred with each other. Yet Runcorne retained sufficient control of himself not to make the mistake of coming too close to Mark or Bragg. Unless Mark missed his guess, the saloonkeeper knew more than a little about gun-handling. Enough to make taking fool chances a mighty dangerous proposition.

"Maybe I'll get some answers when my boys start asking the questions," Runcorne hissed.

"Two of them already tried," Mark pointed out, nodding to the first pair of bouncers as they lay groaning at the sides of the room.

"These two have an advantage," Runcorne replied, making a small but significant gesture with his revolver. "I'm on hand to slow you two down a mite." He paused to let the words sink in. "All right, what're you doing down here?"

"That's a real good question," came Murat's voice from the head of the stairs and he stepped into view. "Put up the gun, Runcorne."

"Damn it, sheriff, I caught this pair down here———"

"Like we-all told the gent, when the fussing started upstairs we just natural-like come down here out of harm's way," Bragg drawled. "Us being such' peaceable souls and all."

"I can see *that*," Murat said dryly, having examined the door and noted the signs of forced entry. "Put up that pint-sized hawg-leg, Mr. Runcorne—as a special favor to me."

Slowly and reluctantly, Runcorne slid the Colt Police Pistol across into its holster under the left side of his jacket. Even if he did not know that Murat distrusted him, the use of the word "mister" would have served as a warning. A Texan only said that word when he disliked an acquaintance. So Runcorne obeyed the order and awaited developments.

A shrewd peace officer, Murat suspected Runcorne of being involved in illegal activities of various kinds but lacked proof. Coming to help the town marshal's deputies break up the fight, he saw Runcorne leading two bouncers into the cellar. The sight aroused Murat's interest and sent him across the room to investigate. He wanted to learn why the saloonkeeper had considered the cellar's contents so valuable that he'd ignored the damage to the barroom. More than that, the saloonkeeper had taken along his two toughest bouncers when they could hardly be spared from their work in quelling the brawl. Finding that the door had been kicked open added to Murat's desire to learn more. On seeing Mark and Bragg in the cellar, he felt that at last there might be a chance to nail Runcorne's hide to the wall.

Watching Murat come down the stairs, Runcorne scowled. The mention of the wine's quality rang a warning bell for him. If the intruders knew something about the barrels' contents—and their presence hinted that they might—he did not want the matter brought up in Murat's hearing.

"They could be telling the truth, sheriff," he said. "Anyways, there's no harm been done."

"Except for the way the door was opened," Murat answered. "It takes a strong man to do it, and one trained as a peace officer. All right, Mark, what brought you pair down here?"

"Maybe Tule told you the truth."

"And maybe he didn't. You pair wouldn't run out on the chance of a fight without good reason."

"We thought we'd got it," Mark admitted. "A feller passed word to me that Runcorne'd been trading guns and whisky for silver with the Kaddos and that it tied into Sam's death, so we came along to see if the story was true."

"*Me* trading with the Indians?" yelped Runcorne in a tone oozing with contemptuous indignation. "That's likely, isn't it?"

"The proof's in the whisky barrels," Mark said.

"Is it, Mr. Runcorne?" asked Murat.

"There's only one way to find out," the saloon-keeper answered and walked across to the barrels. Taking a wooden dipper from the top of the first, he held it under and turned on the tap. Liquid trickled down into the dipper and he offered it to the sheriff. "Taste the proof."

"It's wine all right" Murat said, after obeying, and he sounded a mite disappointed. "How about the other two?"

Watching the saloonkeeper's face, Mark noticed a glint of self-satisfied amusement creep across it. Certainly Runcorne exhibited no concern as he went to the next keg, turned on its tap and filled the dipper with more of the red fluid. After allowing Mark and Murat to taste the contents, Runcorne walked across to the last keg. Once again a flow of wine filled the dipper and the mocking expression grew broader on the saloonkeeper's features.

"It looks like you heard wrong, Mark," Murat stated after sampling the wine from the last barrel.

"It sure looks that way," agreed Mark. "I wouldn't've thought you'd sell much wine, Mr. Runcorne."

In general the Texas cowhand stuck to whisky and beer, leaving the drinking of wine to Mexicans, town dwellers and others with educated thirsts.

"I ship it East, or to the coast," Runcorne answered cheerfully. "Are you satisfied that I'm not peddling firewater and guns to the Indians now?"

Everything about Runcorne's attitude struck Mark as being wrong. Every instinct he possessed told him that Belle's information had been correct. A man in fear of death, desperately trying to buy his life, would not lie. Nor would Belle have risked capture by returning to the hotel unless she believed that Jacobs told her the truth. In addition, the saloon-keeper acted just a mite too sure of himself. Runcorne had the air of a man who brought off a mighty slick bluff at poker. Yet he showed concern at first hearing Mark mention the wine barrels. If they were, as now seemed obvious, filled with wine, he did not need to worry.

"How about it, Mark?" demanded Murat, cutting into the blond giant's flow of thought.

"Who told you that wild story, friend?" asked Runcorne.

"Yeah, Mark, who told you?" Murat went on.

"A reliable source, most times," Mark answered.

"Reliable!" snorted Runcorne. "You tell us his name———"

"A smart feller like you should know better than ask that," Mark replied. "Let's get going, Jules."

"I reckon I ought to be told who started this pack of lies about me, sheriff!" Runcorne insisted. "If it's one of my business rivals I've a right to protect myself, don't I?"

"Like I said," Mark drawled. "A feller who can be relied on, most times."

With that he walked slowly and casually to where several small kegs of whisky were stacked against the wall. Reaching down, he raised one of the top kegs in his two hands.

A mocking sneer crossed Runcorne's face. "You don't reckon I've got that stuff hid in those kegs, do y———?" he began.

The words chopped off as Mark turned, swung up the keg and hurled it at the front of the rightside wine barrel. Wood cracked and splintered under the impact and whisky spurted from the stove-in surface of the keg—but no wine gushed out the barrel. Instead its front sank inward.

An explosive grunt left Murat's lips at the sight. As the upper part of the front tilted into the barrel, its lower edge automatically came out. Fitted to the inside of the front and connected to its tap was a one-gallon keg of wine. The rest of the space held nothing but a number of stone whisky jugs. The sight so surprised Murat that for once he forgot caution. Without taking time to look at Runcorne's party, he started to walk in the direction of the barrel.

Probably Runcorne had no intention of making trouble. The mere possession of the whisky and other items in the remaining barrels was not, in itself, proof of illegal trading with the Indians. It was unlikely that a court would convict him just on that. At the worst he would be told to sell up his place and get out of Austin. So what happened stemmed from one of his men failing to grasp the situation correctly.

Letting out a snarl of rage, the bouncer grabbed out his gun. Bragg flung himself forward, cannoning into the sheriff's back and staggering him aside even as the bouncer's gun cracked. The bullet aimed at Murat's back missed its mark and instead raked a furrow across Bragg's shoulders.

While Runcorne would have cheerfully strangled the bouncer for acting in such a way, he realized what must be done. Knowing that Murat and the two intruders would assume his employee had acted under his orders, he did the only thing left for him to do. Across lashed his hand to where the Colt Police Pistol rode in its butt-forward holster.

Just as Mark guessed, Runcorne was very fast. Not that Mark wasted time in self-congratulation over his shrewd judgment of character. Instead he flung himself backward in the opposite direction to which Bragg had thrust Murat and, in going, sent his hands diving toward the butts of his Colts. Fast though Mark might be, other things stood in Runcorne's favor. The Colt Police Pistol had been designed as a weapon for peace officers to carry concealed; .36 caliber, it had only a three-and-a-half-inch barrel which meant four-and-a-half inches less to clear the holster lip than had Mark's Army Colt. So the saloonkeeper's gun left leather even as Mark's fingers closed on the ivory handles of his Colts.

Out whisked Runcorne's revolver but he made the

fatal mistake of hesitating. While taken by surprise, Murat still started to draw while staggering from Bragg's push. Despite his wound, the foreman also reached for a weapon, grabbing down at the Dance's worn butt with commendable speed. Small wonder that the saloonkeeper showed indecision in the face of three possible threats to his life. Against a man of Mark's ability such vacillation was fatal.

Flame ripped from the barrel of Mark's right-hand Colt as it lined on the saloonkeeper. An instant before Runcorne decided to concentrate first on Mark, the blond giant's bullet caught him between the eyes. Mark shot the only way he dare under the circumstances. Against a man of Runcorne's ability there could be no hesitation in placing the bullet where it would kill instantly. Even so, despite being thrown backward by the impact, Runcorne got off a shot which narrowly missed Mark's head.

Landing on the floor, Murat cut loose on the bouncer who'd started the gunplay. Caught in the chest by a bullet, the man spun around, let his revolver drop, collided with his companion and then slid to the floor. Finding himself covered by Bragg's old Dance, the second bouncer hastily raised his hands and yelled that he was not making any fuss.

The rear entrance's door jerked upward and one of the guards looked in. Seeing what had happened, he started to raise his gun. Rolling over to face the door, Mark made sure that it offered a fresh menace to his friends' well-being and then took steps to counter the threat. The sight of the lined gun and lack of a badge told him that Runcorne's guard and not one of the deputies looked in, so he threw a shot which struck the edge of the door and sent up a cloud of splinters. The man jerked back, letting the door fall down into place. However, he had seen the sheriff and noticed his boss sprawled on the floor. So he called off further attempts at hostilities.

"Close," Murat said, coming to his feet as two

deputy marshals appeared at the head of the stairs. "Thanks, Tule."

"That was a fool trick you pulled," Bragg answered and winced as a movement caused his wound to throb. "Damn it, I'm shot."

Thrusting away his Colt, Mark sprang to Bragg's side and knelt by him. However the foreman let out an explosive snort and pointed. "See if Runcorne can talk. I'll last a mite longer."

"How is it upstairs?" Murat asked the deputies and, on learning the fight had been brought under control, ordered them to attend to the wounded men. Then he turned to Mark. "Let's take a look at the barrels."

Seeing that the deputy seemed competent to care for Bragg until the doctor arrived, Mark accompanied Murat to the wine barrels. They examined the neat way in which Runcorne gave the impression that the barrels held wine.

"It's a pity that Runcorne can't do any talking," the sheriff remarked as he kicked at the front of the center barrel. "Not that I blame you for stopping him, Mark. He was a good man with a gun."

"Sure," Mark answered. "Maybe some of his men can give us the answer."

Before questioning Runcorne's staff, Mark and Murat opened the other two barrels. In one they found a number of Winchester rifles and ammunition, while the other held sacks containing raw silver.

"It's been stored a long time from the way it looks," Murat remarked as he opened one sack.

"So I heard," Mark replied. "The feller allowed it came from some old Spanish mine the Kaddo found."

"You'd best tell me as much as you can," Murat suggested, knowing that only in the most exceptional circumstances would a man like Mark divulge the name of an informant who gave confidential information.

"There's not much to tell. Like I said, word came to me that Runcorne was trading with the Kaddo and that it tied in to Sam's killing. The Wycliffes were waiting for Runcorne's man, who fitted Sam's description enough for them to make a mistake. So I allowed to see if it was true. Reckoned to make Runcorne talk, tell me where the silver came from. That way I'd have a start at finding the Wycliffes should we miss picking up their tracks."

"It was mighty lucky, that fight starting when it did," Murat commented. "You'd never've kicked open the door if all Runcorne's men hadn't been busy with it. Yes sir, Mark, mighty lucky."

"Sure was," agreed Mark. "And to show how grateful I am for being so lucky, I'll pay any fines the gents up there might get."

"It'd be best," said the sheriff judiciously. "What's up with you?"

The last came as the unwounded bouncer moved closer, darted a glance at the first pair, his wounded companion, winked at Murat and nodded in the direction of the stairs. At the sheriff's words, the bouncer showed some agitation and again gazed hurriedly at the other saloon employees. Relief showed on his face as he realized the others did not notice his actions.

"Can we talk?" the bouncer asked in a low tone.

"Go to it," Murat answered.

"Not here, someplace where I'll not be seen doing it," the bouncer said.

"All right," Murat replied in a loud voice. "Show us Runcorne's office."

"Sure, sheriff," agreed the bouncer, trying to sound reluctant. "Come this way."

On arrival at Runcorne's office and with the door safely closed, the reason for the bouncer's agitation became obvious. He wished to betray certain of his late boss's secrets, but not in the presence of the other members of the staff. While Runcorne was undoubtedly dead, the man wanted to continue working in saloons and had no desire to become known as one who told tales to the law.

Not that the man knew much beyond the fact that his employer had traded, through a man called Pegler, with the Kaddo Indians. Pegler would collect the trade goods at night in exchange for sacks of silver, beyond that the bouncer knew nothing. However he bought his freedom to leave Austin, along with Murat's demand that the departure be immediate, with his information. The sheriff showed no sign of it, but he knew something of Pegler.

"He runs a small trading post out on the headwaters of the Pedernales," Murat told Mark after a relieved bouncer left the office.

"That'll be a good place to start happen the trail peters out," Mark replied.

"For you, maybe. But it's well beyond the county line and I've no jurisdiction out there," Murat pointed out. "I'll come along if you need me."

"Thanks, Jules," Mark said. "But you're needed here. Reckon Tejas'll go with me?"

"I reckon he might, but that's the fringe of the Kaddo country."

"I'm still going," Mark stated. "I aim to have the bastards who killed Sailor Sam—even if I have to fight the whole damned Kaddo nation to get them."

CHAPTER TEN

The Coming of the Ysabel Kid

THE white stallion made a magnificent sight. At least a full sixteen hands in height, yet so perfectly proportioned that it moved with swift and easy grace. It might have been a wild creature, despite the bridle and low-horned, double-girthed saddle it bore, for it moved with an air of constant alertness. Not the tense watchfulness, ready to flee at the first hint of hostile sound or scent, that a whitetail deer or broomtail mare showed, but the constant readiness of a master animal willing to fight for its right to survive.

Nor did the man sitting the saddle distract in any way from the stallion's untamed appearance. Six-foot tall, his lean frame gave an impression of whip-cord strength and whang leather toughness. He had a handsome face, almost babyishly young and innocent in feature, if one discounted the wild red-hazel eyes and an Indian-dark tan. At first glance one might take him to be in his early teens. Closer inspection warned that his looks were deceptive; or if he was in his early teens, they had been very hard years. A black Stetson hat of Texas style sat on his raven-dark head of hair. The black motif ran through his entire outfit, bandana, shirt, pants, boots and gunbelt all being of that somber hue. Only the brown walnut grips of the old Dragoon Colt holstered butt

forward at his right side and the ivory hilt of the
James Black bowie knife sheathed on his left hip
relieved the blackness. The butt of a Winchester
Model 1866 rifle showed from his saddleboot and his
armament did not end there.

In his right hand, augmenting the Indian air he
gave in appearance and in the way he rode, was a
Comanche war lance. Its seven-foot-long handle of
bois d'arc wood supported a thirty-inch head of
finely tempered steel. Painted with medicine symbols
and decorated by a cluster of eagle feathers, the lance
looked what it was: a deadly efficient fighting
weapon.

Man and horse made a good pair. Between them
they exhibited an aura of wolf-cautious alertness, the
kind of air a full-grown grizzly bear showed when
crossing its selected territory.

All the time as he rode, the young-looking man
watched the range around him with eyes that missed
little. He saw the distant rump-flashing of a startled
pronghorn start off other flickering signals from its
kind. Near at hand a prairie falcon rose from the
body of a jack rabbit and winged clear of the approaching man. Then he slowed the horse, reared up
in the stirrups and looked ahead. Most men could
have seen only a patch of brown on the rolling green
of the range, but the rider knew he looked at a very
important segment of Texas' major industry: a trail
herd bedded down for the night. On riding closer he
made out the chuck and bed wagons halted in an advantageous position, and the smaller mass of the
remuda which supplied fresh mounts for the men
who worked the cattle.

Feeling that he might like to spend the night in
human company, the rider pointed his stallion
toward the distant herd and allowed it to make better
time in the new direction. All the time he rode, he
studied the night camp. There were a few Texas out-

fits who would not make him welcome and he did not wish to force his company on any man. Before he covered half the distance, he knew that he rode toward friends.

Gathered about the fire while waiting for the cook to start serving the inevitable beef stew and beans, the trail crew watched the approaching rider. One of them, a brash youngster making his first drive north, grinned broadly as he studied the newcomer's armament and gave particular attention to the war lance.

"Damnit!" he grinned to the grizzled veteran at his side. "A war-whoop's done jumped the reservation."

"Was I you, I wouldn't say it so's he could hear you," counseled the other.

"Why not?" demanded the youngster truculently.

"Because that feller's a particular good friend of Big Ranse for one thing," the oldster explained. "And iffen that's not enough, he's also the Ysabel Kid."

Maybe mere loyalty to his employer might not have prevented the youngster making further comment, but the name spoken by the old timer and what went unspoken about it caused him to keep silent. New to the trail, a touch wild and reckless on occasion, the young cowhand possessed sufficient, good common sense not to play games with that babyishly innocent-looking rider.

Many knowledgeable people claimed the Ysabel Kid to be the most dangerous member of Ole Devil Hardin's floating outfit. True, he could not equal either Dusty Fog's or Mark Counter's speed on the draw, although he performed passably well with his old Dragoon Colt in time of necessity. His talent in the skilled use of the bowie knife made up for any close-range deficiencies with a handgun and his marksmanship when using the rifle almost passed belief. Yet those attributes alone did not make him one to be feared.

Born of an Irish–Kentuckian father and French Creole–Comanche mother, the Kid spent his rearing years among the *Pehnane* band of his mother's tribe. From his maternal grandfather, Chief Long Walker, he learned those things a Comanche warrior needed to know.* He could ride any horse ever foaled, follow tracks where lesser men might see nothing, move in silence through any kind of country, hide and locate hidden enemies; and he knew the ways of the great Texas plains. Less of a cowhand than his two companions, he acted as scout in time of danger. So the talents taught to make him a brave-heart warrior found many uses among the white men.

After seeing his grandfather's people settled on their new home and satisfying himself that the word of the White Father in Washington would be kept to the *Pehnane*, the Kid began his journey to the OD Connected. On his way he had to deliver the war lance to the governor of Texas, being both a tribute to the man who made the peace possible and a sign that the Wasps, Raiders, Quick Stingers—those names being the nearest white equivalent to *Pehnane*—rode no more to war. Cheerfully he rode toward the trail drive's camp, knowing he could expect hospitality from Big Ranse Counter's crew.

Mark's father equaled him in size and muscular development, although age had put thickness to Big Ranse's middle. Dressed like a working cowhand, with an Army Colt hanging at his side, the rancher swung away from the bed wagon and raised his hand in greeting to the newcomer.

"Howdy, Kid. This wouldn't be some of your Comanche witchcraft, would it?"

* Told in *Comanche*.

"How's that?" asked the Kid.

"You've sure showed up at the right time."

"For what?"

"Mark's likely to need help."

"Where and for what?"

Forgotten was the visit to Austin and presentation of the war lance to the governor. The Kid's face showed little, but interest glinted in his red-hazel eyes as he listened to Ranse Counter's story of the happenings in the capital. Just a hint of worry began to show on the Indian-dark features as Ranse told how the Wycliffe gang's tracks had been lost but that Mark went on with the search.

"Just him and Tejas Tom went on," the rancher concluded. "They're headed up the Pedernales River toward Pegler's place."

"That's on the edge of the Kaddo country," the Kid breathed, thinking of a story going the rounds of the *Pehnane* camp before he left it.

"And he'll not stop there if the Wycliffes've gone on," Ranse continued. "I'm fixing to go after him."

"How about your herd?" asked the Kid.

"That's just what I've been asking the old goat!" yelled a peevish voice from the bed wagon and Bragg thrust his head into sight. "I've got all shot 'n' can't ride trail boss. There's fifteen hundred head of our stuff and another thousand for two other spreads bedded down back there that he has to get to market."

With beef prices at the Kansas rail head standing high, that amounted to a tolerable sum of money. Far too much to be tossed aside without real good reason. Not that the financial considerations worried Ranse Counter with his son in danger, but the Kid guessed that the other two spreads relied upon the rancher to take the herd through. So the Kid reached his decision fast, knowing that Ole Devil Hardin would expect him to act in such a manner.

"Let me go after him," the Kid suggested. "I can travel faster than you, and faster alone than if you come with me."

For a long moment Ranse Counter hesitated and digested the Kid's words. All too well he knew the close ties which bound the floating outfit's members, so realized that every effort would be made to reach Mark in time and back his play no matter how great the odds. The Kid's timely arrival presented the best possible answer to Ranse's problem. While the rancher had fully intended to ride to his son's aid, he knew the penalty for doing so. He could survive the loss of the herd, but two neighbors depended on him to deliver and sell their cattle, providing them with badly needed money to carry them through until the next year.

Knowing the Kid's reputation, Ranse had no doubt in the other's ability to find Mark. Also the Kid spoke the simple truth when he stated that he could travel faster alone.

"Go to it, Lon," the rancher ordered. "Is there anything you want?"

"Reckon I've everything I need," the Kid replied. "Can you send my war bag into Austin; I'll be traveling light."

"I'll see to it for you," Ranse promised.

Dawn found the Kid in the saddle, although his bedroll no longer rode on the cantle. All he carried besides his clothing were bullets for the rifle, a powder horn and twenty ready-molded balls to be used in the Dragoon, his knife and the war lance. To his way of thinking the latter did not form added weight, but was his passport into the Kaddo camp should one be needed.

Being a white man, Ranse Counter would have ridden down river from his camp at the junction of the Llando and Colorado, followed the edge of Lake Travis to where the Pedernales flowed into it and up the latter stream. Not so the Kid. Using his inborn sense of direction, he proposed to ride across country at an angle that would bring him to the headwaters of the Pedernales. Doing so would save time and, he hoped, bring him to the vicinity of the Pegler trading post ready to back up Mark on the blond giant's arrival.

The route taken by the Kid took him through country not yet occupied by rancher or town dweller. For all that he lived well, relying on his rifle to supply meat and augmenting it with fruits or nuts and the tuberous roots of the Indian potato. Despite the urgency of the situation, he ensured that both he and the horse ate well. He knew that he traveled faster than Mark could while following tracks and on a route that he hoped would converge with the other's before arrival at the trading post.

For two days the Kid rode over the rolling Texas range without the sight or trace of another human being. He had covered over forty miles the first day and figured to be coming close to his destination. However, search the horizon as he might, he saw no smoke rising from the trading post's chimney nor distant glint of the sun reflected from the building's windows.

The rapid drumming of hooves came to the Kid's ears from beyond the rim up which he rode. At the same moment the wind, coming from the direction of the sound, carried a scent to the white stallion's nostrils, setting it fiddle-footing nervously and snorting as if to blow away the offending odor. Reading the signs correctly, despite the lack of confirmatory noise, the Kid started his horse moving up to the head of the rim. While he knew roughly what to expect, the sight before him brought a deep-throated exclamation bursting from his lips and caused him to bring the stallion to an abrupt halt.

Anywhere west of the Mississippi River, especially

on the open ranges of Texas, the sight of a saddled, riderless horse gave rise to concern. Yet not even the sight of eight wolves loping after the fleeing horse at the foot of the valley beyond the rim added to the shock received by the Kid. That wolves hunted so large an animal did not surprise him. He knew they would take after any creature offering the possibility of a meal when hunger gnawed at them. What caused the Kid to sit back and take notice was the fact that he recognized the fleeing horse.

There might be other huge blood bay stallions in Texas, probably most of them would carry a similar style of saddle—the low-horned, double-girthed rig being much favored by sons of the Lone Star State—but the Kid suffered from no doubts. He knew the horse to be Mark's favorite mount and could have picked it out from a big remuda.

Although the sight of Mark's riderless horse handed the Kid one hell of a shock, it did not freeze him into panic-filled immobility. Letting the lance fall from his right hand, he tossed his right leg across the front of the saddle and dropped to the ground. In passing he slid the rifle from its boot and his eyes measured the distance separating him from the horse. The rifle carried a slide rear sight graduated from one hundred to nine hundred yards. Loyal supporter of Oliver F. Winchester's product though he might be, the Kid admitted the upper graduations on the sight's scale were no more than wishful thinking. Twenty-eight grains of even the best powder could not propel the two hundred-grain bullet nine hundred yards with any hope of hitting its intended target. However the horse and wolves came along the valley bottom in his direction and at much less than a quarter of a mile.

Even as he sank to his left knee and rested his left elbow on the bent right leg, the Kid knew he had no time to spare if he hoped to save the horse. As if sensing the danger of an intervention between it and the pack's prey, the big dog wolf in the lead increased its speed. Like most of the other species of its kind, the medium-sized, dark grey-colored, comparatively thincoated Texas grey wolf could lope along at a speed of ten to twelve miles an hour for long periods. At a spurt, it might touch more than twice that speed. The dog wolf put on such a spurt, closing on the racing blood bay with the intention of chopping at the tendons of the lower leg. A bite there would hamstring the horse, bring it to a halt and leave it at the mercy of the pack.

The Kid did not take time to raise and adjust the leaf sight. At such a short range he could use the ordinary V notch sight and allow for deviations of distance. Swiftly he sighted, right forefinger curled around the trigger and starting to take the pressure. Even as the wolf gathered itself for the final leap, the Winchester cracked. Drilled through the chest, the wolf uttered a shrill help and somersaulted over. Down and up blurred the rifle's lever, throwing out the empty cartridge case and replacing it with a loaded bullet. The Kid changed aim and sent his next bullet through the shoulders of the second wolf, tumbling it under the feet of the remainder of the pack. Again he fired, sending lead into the wolves as they halted, snarling and tearing at their fallen companions.

Even in an area far from human habitation, the wolves knew what the sound of a rifle meant. So they did not stick around to face more of the Kid's lead. Pulling away from the shot animal at which they mauled, the five unwounded wolves raced off at such speed that trying to shoot them would have been a waste of lead.

Booting his rifle, the Kid darted around his horse. The big white had stood like a statue, ignoring the crack of the rifle, smell of burning powder and scent of the wolves. Nor did it make a move until after the

Kid, scooping up the lance in passing, bounded afork the saddle. Urged forward by its master, the white started down the slope in the direction of the fleeing blood bay.

Ridden by a man trained from his earliest days in the business of staying astride a horse, the white went down the slope at a good speed. Once on the level floor of the valley bottom, it really stretched out and showed how it could run. Crouching lightly in the saddle, the Kid used all his considerable skill to help the white. All too well he knew the speed at which Mark's blood bay could travel. While the white could run faster, it carried more weight than the blood bay and so needed every aid its rider offered.

Fear kept the blood bay running, but it had been pushed hard and long by the wolves. For all that, a quarter of a mile fell behind them before the Kid's white caught up. Grunting out a curse, the Kid thrust the lance under his left leg to leave his hands free. Slowly the white drew level with the other horse. Looking across, he saw the reins looped around the saddlehorn. Like the Kid, Mark could rely on his horse to stand without tying for a short time. Something must have spooked the blood bay and set it running after Mark left it. The Kid wanted to learn what the something had been.

Leaning across, the Kid gripped the blood bay's reins. A knee signal caused his white to slow down and between them they brought the other horse to a halt. The Kid retained his hold as he dropped from the saddle. On landing, he set to work to calm the blood bay so that he could examine it closer.

"Easy, big feller," he said gently. "Easy there."

The Kid's familiar scent, mingled with his voice and firm, capable handling swiftly brought the horse under control. Although badly blown and heavily lathered by the wolves' long chase, the blood bay yielded no immediate sign of damage. After making

sure that another flight would not be the result of letting go of the reins, the Kid examined its right side.
Alert for any sign of restlessness, he passed around
the horse's rump. Then he saw the reddish tint of the
lather on the left hip and went closer to investigate.

Gently, the Kid placed a finger on the discolored
patch, meaning to clean away the lather. He felt the
horse quiver and spoke softly to calm it before continuing. Underneath the coating of lather he found a
shallow graze in the skin. Bending closer and wiping
off more of the froth sweated out during the chase,
he saw that the hair had been burned away at the
start of the groove. One did not need the powers of a
Comanche witch woman to guess at the cause. Somebody had cut loose with a revolver at close range, the
muzzle-blast singed the blood bay and the bullet
sliced a nick in its flank. Pain started it running and
somewhere in its flight it attracted the attention of
the wolves. Luckily the wound had been only super-
ficial or the pack would have pulled the blood bay
down long before it came into the Kid's sight.

Glancing toward the horse's head, the Kid's eyes
came to a halt at the saddle. He saw a dark stain on
the leather and, hoping against hope, he moved
closer to check the evidence of his eyes. Shock and
anxiety twisted at his usually unemotional face as he
looked at the stain. All too well he knew what the
dark mark was, human blood. Far worse, he iden-
tified the greyish lumps which clung to the leather
among the bloodstain. Blood and human brains had
been smeared down the saddle. The Kid looked back
in the direction from which the blood bay came and
tried not to think that the hideous stain might
originate from Mark Counter's shattered-open skull.

CHAPTER ELEVEN

Sandel's Gratitude

CAREFUL searching had located the tracks of the Wycliffe gang and Murat's small posse had followed until they had reached the border of Travis County. By that time they had reached the shores of Lake Travis and found that the gang had crossed the Pedernales River to turn upstream along the northern bank. When Mark had stated his intention of continuing the hunt, Murat had offered to accompany him, although the sheriff's jurisdiction ended at the county line. While Mark and Murat discussed the matter, a rider from Austin galloped up with news. It seemed that the Dick Dublin gang had been seen at Williamson and rode out of that town in the direction of Austin. The town marshal of Williamson believed Dublin planned a robbery in the state capital. Even if he did not, Dublin's name appeared on sufficient wanted posters to make his capture a matter of some importance. As county sheriff, senior law enforcement officer of the area, Murat would be needed. Knowing the reputation of the Dublin gang, Murat did not want to face them with casual help and required the services of all his deputies. That left just Mark and Tejas Tom to follow Wycliffe's party.

The young Indian came from a tribe long noted for its friendship to the white man. As Murat said, his clothing meant little for underneath lay the primitive instincts and knowledge of the red warrior. Throughout the trailing of the gang Mark had studied Tejas and knew him to be capable and skilled at his work.

Once again refusing to take men Murat might need to handle the Dublin gang, Mark turned his blood bay stallion across the river. Tejas, cradling a tack-decorated Spencer carbine across his arm, followed and then led the way on the tracks of Wycliffe's bunch.

After a time Mark concluded that the bouncer at the Lone Rider had told the truth. Wycliffe's gang had swung away from the river only to avoid contact with the occasional settler's home. Once past the dwelling, the gang had returned to the river trail.

During the afternoon Tejas pointed out where a further six riders had joined the Wycliffe party.

"That makes maybe twelve of 'em." Mark said, glancing at the Indian.

"More than we figure on," Tejas answered.

"You want to go back?"

"Are you going on?"

"Sure," admitted Mark.

"I took on to find 'em for you," Tejas pointed out. "Not done it yet."

"Let's go then," Mark drawled.

They started their horses moving once more, finding no difficulty in following the other party even though Wycliffe had stuck to the trail most of the time. Two miles farther upstream the trail petered out, having grown narrower and less used after each settler's buildings. Still the gang had stuck close to the river, until they had made camp for the night.

"They split up here this morning," Tejas explained after circling the camp and reading tracks in the light of the setting sun. "Look like they spread out, four bunches of them."

That figured, thinking of the Army map Mark had studied before leaving Austin. Discounting the usual twists and bends, the Pedernales River formed a rough crescent from its source in what would one day form the eastern edge of Kimble County and where it entered Lake Travis. If Pegler knew the country, he might avoid the extra miles caused by following the windings of the river and take a direction line from the headwaters to Austin. So Wycliffe split up his party, spreading them out across the range in the hope that one group might see the trader.

Which left Mark with a problem.

"Who do we follow?" he asked.

"These three took girl with 'em." Tejas answered, indicating the set of tracks which pointed along the bank of the river.

"Was Billy with them?" Mark asked.

"His hoss tracks go with 'em," Tejas agreed.

"Then they're for us," the blond giant growled. "I'll be satisfied if I can nail his hide to the wall."

"They not make such fast time with girl along," commented Tejas. "Not try hide their tracks either. Maybe so we catch 'em tomorrow."

"Let's push on as far as we can today," Mark suggested.

That proved to be another mile, by which time the sun had set and night came blackly to the land. Much as Mark liked his creature comforts—his habit of including a comfortable pillow in his bed roll when on the trail had been the cause of amused comment—he accepted that the conditions called for making a very primitive camp that night. They settled the horses on good grazing but limited themselves to drinking river water and eating the cold food brought from Austin, not even troubling to make a fire. Then Mark settled down to sleep, using his saddle for a pillow, the earth forming a hard, unsatisfactory mattress and the sky a roof.

Just how long Mark had been asleep he did not know. At the first gentle shake Tejas gave his arm, he came immediately and silently awake.

"I heard something," the Indian said. "Listen!"

Sitting up, Mark strained his ears. At first he heard nothing but the normal night sounds. Then it came, the scream of a terrified woman mingled with whoops, laughter and voices.

"Not white men!" Tejas breathed, reaching the same conclusion as Mark.

"Let's go take a look," the blond giant replied.

Even as he spoke a further scream rose, to be chopped off as if a hand clamped over the woman's mouth. Taking up their rifles, Mark and Tejas moved swiftly through the trees in the direction of the sounds. The country bordering that part of the Pedernales River lay in thickly wooded rolling folds. It was an area not well suited to the raising of cattle, one of the reasons for the sparse population; also, the U.S. Cavalry did not maintain regular patrols through the district. So Mark and Tejas did not discount the possibility of finding hostile Indians responsible for the screams. Not until they topped the second ridge from their camp did either man see any sign of other human beings.

Shapes moved about a large fire in a clearing down close to the river. Even from where they stood Mark and Tejas could make out sufficient details to tell them that they must intervene—and also enough to warn them that doing so would involve some risk.

Swiftly Mark counted the Indian ponies he could see standing at the far side of the clearing on the edge of the firelight. He made the score then, not taking in the four horses of better breeding than the small, wiry broomtails. Ten corresponded with the braves around the fire. Six of that number helped themselves to liberal doses from a brace of stone whisky jugs. The remaining quartet appeared to be engrossed in preparations for entertaining their companions, with the unwilling aid of at least one of their prisoners.

Close to the horses, bound to a tree and with a stick forced into her mouth as a gag, was a blonde-haired girl clad in a man's shirt which had lost one sleeve and Levi's pants. Just as securely fastened, although not gagged, the lanky form of a man in range clothes lay by the fire. Mark needed only one glance to identify the prisoner as Loney Sandel, one of Wycliffe's companions from the saloon.

After studying the camp, Mark turned his attention back to the quartet of industrious braves. All the party wore a mixture of traditional and white man's clothing, while three sported gunbelts and revolvers. Three of the quartet appeared to be laying a second fire, for they piled dried leaves and small branches on the ground beneath a tall old white oak tree. Taking up a rope, the fourth buck flipped its noose end over a branch directly above where his companions built the new fire. Mark could guess what the quartet had in mind.

Whooping their delight, the three braves left their work and crossed to where Sandel lay. Like Mark, the lanky man knew what the Indians planned and began to throw his body from side to side in a vain attempt to free his arms. He achieved nothing other than to bring whoops and laughter from the watching braves. Grabbing him by his bound ankles, the trio of braves hauled him bodily to the oak tree. The fourth buck, with Sandel's gunbelt and Cooper Navy revolvers slung about his waist, deftly flipped the noose over the prisoner's feet and drew it tight about his ankles. Watched by the remainder of the party, the three braves sprang to the other end of the rope and began hauling at it. Laughter and shouted advice rose from the watching warriors as Sandel's body started to rise feet first into the air.

"Young Kaddo bucks!" Tejas whispered as he and Mark advanced down the slope.

"Looks that way," Mark agreed. "We'll have to jump them fast or they'll kill the girl."

"Noise they're making, they'll not hear us come," Tejas guessed.

Certainly none of the braves showed any hint of knowing, or caring, that they had been discovered. They laughed, whooped, yelled comments to each other. Hauling on the rope, the trio drew it up and over the branch until they suspended Sandel head downward over the mound of inflammable material. Then the fourth buck darted to the fire and dragged out a blazing branch. Waving it over his head, he started back across the clearing.

While Mark would have preferred to be much closer before cutting in, he did not dare wait any longer. Sandel might be one of the crowd who helped kill Sailor Sam but the blond giant could not stand by and watch him tortured. In addition to his revulsion at the thought of a man being hung head down over a fire, Mark wanted to question Sandel and learn if Billy Wycliffe owned one of the riderless horses standing with the Indian ponies. If Billy had died at the hands of the braves, Mark would be willing to call off his hunt. Yet Mark doubted if Billy had fallen victim to the Kaddo braves. None of them wore a gunbelt with a swivel holster.

Skidding to a halt, Mark swung the Winchester rifle to his shoulder and took aim at the brave with the blazing branch. When sure of his aim, the blond giant squeezed the trigger. Flame lanced through the darkness and the bullet ripped into the brave's head. Spinning around, he flung the torch aside and tumbled to the ground.

So engrossed in the forthcoming torture were the rest that the shot came as a complete surprise. Nor did their whisky-slowed minds take in what the sound meant with any kind of speed. On the heels of Mark's shot, Tejas' Spencer bellowed to crumple over one of the men holding the rope. Sandel's weight dragged the other two braves forward and he had sense enough to curl his body forward as it sank down. In that way he saved himself from injury, landing on the unlit pile of branches and then flopping to the ground.

After ending the immediate threat to Sandel's life, Mark concentrated his efforts on preventing the remaining bucks from recovering from their surprise and organizing a defense. While the Winchester's mechanism enabled a skilled man to get off two shots a second, no amount of practice could teach him to change his point of aim at that speed. So Mark concentrated on sending lead fast and in the general direction of the braves; all the time making the woods ring with bawled-out cowhand yells.

At Mark's side, Tejas showed a remarkably good grasp of the situation and of his companion's intentions. Long before they could render all the braves harmless, the initial shock would have worn off. Maybe the Kaddo did not rank with the Comanche as fighting men, but they could handle their end in a fracas and were not to be despised. Given a brief time to regain control of their startled wits, any of the party left alive would at least kill the two prisoners before being settled. However the need to thumbcock the hammer between shots prevented the Spencer from equaling the Winchester's speed of discharge. So Tejas used the extra time to take aim. He might not be able to put down such a volume of fire as Mark, but he made at least as much vocal disturbance.

Another buck went down, thrown across the fire by the shocking impact of a .52 caliber Spencer bullet. By that time the Kaddos milled about the clearing and Mark did no more than catch a brave high in the shoulder, giving him a bad graze but nothing worse.

Then the rest of the Indians broke. Like many of the Indian tribes, the Kaddo did not care to fight at night. They believed that the Great Spirit might fail to find a dead warrior in the darkness, preventing him from being guided to the Land of Good Hunting. So they raced for their horses, wanting only to escape from their unseen attackers. One of the braves had to pass the girl and snatched the tomahawk from his belt as he approached her. Seeing her danger, Mark swung the barrel of his Winchester and sighted. Rifle and carbine cracked at the same moment. Caught in the head by a .44 caliber bullet and raked through the body by a .52 ball, the Kaddo was a tolerable dead Indian even before his body crashed down at the girl's side.

Showing the kind of skill one expected of horse-Indians, the remainder of the band mounted their ponies. Even the wounded brave hit his mount's back with commendable speed. Nor did they intend to leave such valuable loot as horses in the hands of their attackers. Their own ponies stood with no more than a hackamore tossed across the branch of a bush. Only the captured white men's horses needed fastening and the braves succeeded in cutting free all but one. Lead whistled around their heads, coming close enough to prevent any great effort to sever the fine-looking dun's reins. While that horse was the best of the looted quartet, none of the braves felt like giving his life to free it. Taking all but the dun, the braves fled into the darkness and could be heard crashing off through the trees at speed.

Cautiously Mark and Tejas advanced into the firelight and moved forward to ensure they did not need to worry about the braves lying about the clearing. They held their weapons ready and did not regret the precaution even after it proved to be needless.

"Cut that jasper free, Tejas," Mark ordered. "Then go fetch up our horses. We'd best get the hell out of here."

Although the Kaddo did not fight in the night, the departed bucks might be tempted to return in an effort to retrieve their abandoned property. The discarded whisky jugs alone would form a mighty strong inducement. If the braves returned, they would come in silence and follow their attackers' tactics of cutting loose out of the darkness. There might be more Indians in the vicinity, in which case Mark's party might find themselves faced with greater odds than they could handle. All his and Tejas' spare ammunition had been left with their saddles and Mark wanted a reserve on hand should an attack come.

Even without going into details, Tejas followed Mark's line of thought. Taking a Green River knife from its sheath beneath his jacket, the Indian knelt at Sandel's side. As he started to free the man, Tejas watched his face and the manner in which his eyes followed Mark.

Crossing the clearing, Mark rested his rifle against the tree trunk, took a jackknife from his pocket. First he removed the cruel gag from the girl's mouth. In normal times she would have been a pretty girl, with a freckled face, snub nose and smiling lips. The ordeal she had gone through left marks of terror and exhaustion on her features.

Working fast, Mark cut the girl free and she collapsed sobbing into his arms. Gently he held her, feeling the sobs which tore at her and the uncontrollable trembling of her body against his.

"Easy now," he said quietly. "Just take it easy. It's all over now."

After cutting Sandel's bonds, Tejas turned and

faded off into the darkness. Sitting up, Sandel rubbed at the inside of his wrists and cursed the pain that restored circulation shot through him. Then his eyes returned once more to Mark and verified the identification already made. Most men would have been filled with gratitude for an escape from agonizing death, but Sandel thought only of his future. That future did not look any too bright in view of the identity of the man who had rescued him.

Despite his apologies and professions of good feelings, Churn Wycliffe had taken time to learn the name of his family's assailant before leaving Austin. The Wycliffe clan relied too much on their reputation for salty toughness to mildly accept the kind of treatment handed to them before witnesses in the Bigfoot Saloon. Any plans for extracting retribution had been put off until finishing the business that had brought them to the state capital. More than that, Churn Wycliffe hesitated before making trouble for a member of Ole Devil's floating outfit unless he could select the time and place.

So Wycliffe had led his party out of Austin in search of Trader Pegler. Too late they discovered the mistake they had made when grabbing that bearded jasper and girl. A search of the man's body and his wagon informed them of his name and that he worked as cook for the R over C ranch, owned by Big Ranse Counter, father of the man who had rough-handled three prime members of the Wycliffe bunch.

Which meant that Sandel owed his life to Mark Counter. Maybe Sandel was not bright, but he could guess what brought the blond giant out along the Pedernales River. Even if it be no more than chance, the girl knew everything. She would tell how Billy Wycliffe shot Sailor Sam and mention Sandel's part in the affair. Even if Mark did not more than take Sandel in for trial, the girl's evidence would be damning. Most Texas juries held every member of a gang present to be responsible for the actions of the others. Sandel knew that family influence could not save him if Mark Counter handed him over to the law.

Darting a glance around him, Sandel could see no sign of Tejas and concluded that the Indian had gone to obey Mark's orders. Then his eyes went to the dun horse which still stood tied to a bush. With the horse between his knees Sandel figured he could make good his escape and either join up with the rest of the gang or head for the safety of the San Saba country. Added salvation lay not far from him, in the shape of the brave who had taken his gunbelt when he fell into their hands. The butt of the right-side Cooper revolver stuck up like a signpost directing Sandel to escape from his perilous position.

Slowly and cautiously Sandel inched his way to the Kaddo's body. Mark still stood with his back to the man, comforting the girl and oblivious of his danger. It never occurred to the blond giant that Sandel knew him, or understood his presence in connection with the murder of Sailor Sam. There would be time to deal with Sandel after they put some miles between themselves and the clearing—or so Mark believed. First he must get the girl in a condition where she could stand a hard, fast ride through the night.

Sliding free the Cooper, Sandel used the Kaddo's body as a nest. After being tied for so long, his right hand lacked the strength to control the gun adequately. He knew the penalty of missing, so gripped his right hand in the left and propped them on the immobile flesh of the dead Indian. Running the tip of his tongue across lips which felt suddenly dry, Sandel lined his gun on Mark's back.

While resembling the Navy Colt in a number of external details, including being the same general shape, the Cooper differed from its more famous rival in one major aspect. Being single action, the

Colt must be hand-cocked for each shot. The Cooper offered its user the advantage of operating "double-action"; pressure on its trigger served to carry the hammer back to full cock and then to snap down on to the percussion cap. Sandel only rarely made use of the double-action, preferring to thumb back the hammer. Lining his gun on Mark's back, he squeezed the trigger. To manually cock the hammer gave off an audible click which might reach the blond giant's ears. One could not give chances to a man like Mark Counter without the danger of him taking them with fatal results to the giver.

The shot roared out loud in the stillness of the night. Whirling around, Mark sent his right hand down to its Colt and used the left to grip the girl and thrust her to safety behind the tree should it be necessary. He saw Sandel rear up, let the Cooper fall from limp hands and pitch forward to lie face down across the Kaddo's body.

Smoke curled up lazily from the barrel of Tejas' Spencer as he walked from the trees.

"That one had a bad heart, *amigo*," the Indian said, nodding to Sandel. "I see it in his eyes. Wait among trees and watch him. He tried to kill you."

"*Gracias*," Mark replied. "I should have figured on it. It's a pity. I'd questions I wanted to ask him."

"He not answer you now," Tejas stated, looking at the ruin his bullet made of Sandel's skull. "Bring girl, *amigo*. This is not a good place for us to stay."

CHAPTER TWELVE

The Remains of Pegler's Trading Post

TEJAS insisted Mark check the saddle of the dun. Then, while the Indian appropriated Sandel's gunbelt and Cooper revolvers for his own use, Mark helped the girl on to the horse. Much as he wanted to question her as to the fate of Sandel's companions, one glance told him doing so at that time would be fruitless. Shock and strain rendered the girl incoherent. So, even without the urgent necessity to leave the area, he wanted to take her from the clearing and give her a chance to recover.

Leading the dun, Mark followed Tejas through the trees to their camp. After helping the girl down, the big blond saddled his blood bay. No less swiftly Tejas prepared to leave and led the way through the woodland away from the river. Already satisfied with Tejas' abilities, Mark found the Indian worthy of ranking with the Ysabel Kid in the matter of moving through the darkness. So Mark left the guiding of the party in Tejas' hands, staying by the girl's side to encourage and support her through a four-mile ride.

After falling behind for a time, so as to listen for sounds of pursuit, Tejas caught up with Mark and the girl. He told Mark that they had traveled far enough, but he wished to find a secluded spot in which they could spend the rest of the night. Ranging ahead, Tejas selected a draw with steep walls and a

133

stream flowing along its center.

"This what we want," he told Mark in satisfaction, leading the way between the walls.

By that time the girl seemed on the verge of collapse. She slid limply from her horse as Mark swung out of the blood bay's saddle. Turning, he caught her and set her down on the springy grass.

"Reckon we can chance a fire, Tejas?" he asked. "She's cold, tuckered out and could likely stand some food in her belly."

"Nobody followed us that I could hear," the Indian answered. "Down here we make small fire and not be seen. Have it out before daylight then they not see any smoke. I make-um, you watch girl."

However, the girl seemed over the worst of the shock, so Mark left her and went to tend to the horses. She shuddered, but could think well enough to realize they might need the animals when daylight came. Neglecting their mounts at that moment could easily cost them their lives later, so she made no objections. Sitting on the ground, she hugged her arms about her knees and shuddered at the thought of what the past two days had brought her.

Soon a small fire blazed close to the girl, and her rescuers joined her after removing saddles and seeing to the horses' welfare. While Mark looked after the girl at the clearing, Tejas had taken time to gather various things discarded by the Kaddo which his party could use. It seemed that the Indians hunted with some success and traveled intending to feed well. They had left behind a cooked hindquarter of prime whitetail buck meat, a parfleche-covered slab of pemmican and a cleaned-out buffalo paunch filled with honey. Bringing the food along, Tejas presented his companions with the means of making a good meal. Despite the ordeal she had passed through, the girl ate well and at the end, although tired, seemed to be recovering from the shock.

"Now you just settle down," Mark told her when she finished eating. "We've made up a bed for you and comes morning we'll see about taking you back home."

"Home!" she gasped. "Lordy lord, I never thought I'd want to go back there."

"We'll see you get there, don't worry on that score," Mark assured her. "So just lie down and get some sleep."

The girl shuddered, but obeyed. "After what's happened to me and what I've seen these last couple of days, I doubt if I'll ever sleep again," she groaned as she drew one of Mark's blankets over her.

"Talk then," he suggested. "It'll maybe help you to go to sleep and I'd like to hear how you came to be out here and all."

Slowly the girl's story came out. Her name was Winnie Odville and her folks ran a small place down on the Cibolo River. After hearing traveling men talk about the gay, exciting life in the cities, Winnie had decided to see some of it for herself. Borrowing an older brother's clothes, she took one of the family's plough mules and set out for Austin. On the way to the capital a black bear had spooked her mule and set her afoot. Catching up to her on the trail, Sailor Sam had offered her a ride. He accepted her story that she lived in Austin and had been visiting kin when the mule threw her.

Mark listened patiently to the girl as she began to tell him about her family. While life had been boring and occasionally hard, she no longer wanted to put her home behind her. Instead she wished that she had never left and would be only too pleased to return, even if Paw did whale the tar out of her for losing the mule.

Then she returned to telling him what he wanted to know. He let her tell the story in her own way, knowing that way would give him more than if he pressed questions on her.

Much of what Winnie next told him did no more
than confirm Tejas' reading of the sign. Wycliffe's
men had rode up to the wagon, acting in a friendly
manner until close. Then they had drawn guns and
ordered Sailor Sam to leave the trail. Down by the
river he had attacked his captors in an attempt to let
Winnie escape. Billy Wycliffe had shot the cook in
his rage at having been knocked down.

"That big feller they call Churn went near crazy
wild with Billy," Winnie went on. "I think he'd've
whupped him right there and then only one of the
others said he thought they'd got the wrong man.
And they had. They thought Sam was a trader called
Pegler."

"What happened then?" Mark prompted gently.

"They just left Sam where he lay. I thought they'd
kill me as well, but the big feller said for them to
take me with them—so they took me, went back and
watched the trail—sheriff came, they saw him and a
posse in the distance."

While talking, her eyes fought to stay open. Then
the exhaustion which filled her took over and she
sank into a deep sleep.

"Girl not tell much," Tejas commented.

"Only what we knew," Mark replied. "Likely
we'll get more out of her after she's rested."

The two men settled down once more and spent the
remainder of the night undisturbed. Waking before
daylight broke, Tejas doused the fire and made sure
that no smoke rose from it. The girl slept on for some
time and they let her. While Mark stayed in the draw
to guard her, Tejas slipped off to scout the surrounding country for signs of the Kaddo. He returned
before the girl awoke and brought disturbing news.
Although the braves from the clearing did not appear
to be on their trail, Tejas saw a bunch of maybe a
dozen more passing in a downriver direction.

As the men sat discussing the news, Winnie stirred and sat up rubbing her eyes. Then she seemed to remember where she was and stared at her rescuers for a few moments in panic before realizing who they might be.

"There's only water to drink, but we've still food left," Mark told her.

"Food cold," Tejas went on. "We can't have fire."

Cold venison without salt might be unpalatable, but pemmican, "Indian bread," generously coated with honey rated as a delicacy and more than made up for the deficiencies of the meat. After eating, Mark prompted the girl to start telling her story again. Shaking her head sadly, Winnie cursed the Wycliffes in general and Billy in particular.

"He's a mean one, that," she told the two men. "Why, he just shot old Sam down like I'd swat a fly. And he figured to bad-use me, only his uncle wouldn't let him. That was in camp the night they killed Sam. Next day they got me on a hoss, it was a spare that Sandel feller had along, and made me ride with them. Churn said they daren't wait around with the sheriff on the prowl and they'd go look for Pegler. So they brought me up to that river, crossed it and started going upstream. Then they met another six of his men. All the time Billy kept eyeing me and mauling me. I tell you I was one scared gal until his uncle told him to keep his hands off."

Shuddering, Winnie stopped talking for a short time. Then she regained control of herself and went on with the story. There had been some argument about the best course of action among the men. At last Churn Wycliffe had stated they would split into four parties of three men each. He had also stamped on Billy's suggestion of being the one who escorted Winnie, putting her in the care of Sandel.

During the night Sandel won Billy's dun horse in a poker game, although Churn insisted he loaned the youngster his own mount. The Kaddo braves had ambushed Winnie's party, killing two of the men. Thrown when the dun reared, Sandel had been captured alive along with the girl. After riding a time, the braves made camp for the night. At first they had ignored their prisoners, but decided to have some fun following a drinking session. When she realized the braves' intentions, Winnie screamed and was gagged. The rest Mark knew without her telling.

"What'd Wycliffe tell the others before they split up?" he asked.

"To spread across the range and watch for Pegler and they'd meet up again at the trading post," Winnie replied. "Say, how'd you come to be out this way?"

"I'm looking for the Wycliffes. Sailor Sam worked for my pappy and was a good friend."

"It was Billy killed him———"

"I figure to see Billy about it."

"That big feller, Churn, he didn't want it to happen and he stopped Billy abusing me."

Possibly Wycliffe had acted in a chivalrous manner, but Mark doubted it. More probably the burly man had kept Winnie alive and unharmed for less noble reasons. He could not be sure how soon the law might come after him and did not want the rape or death of a girl added to his crimes. So he kept Billy at bay. Sending Winnie with Sandel showed more cunning than trust in the man. If a posse should be on his party's trail, they would probably follow the group with the girl. Wycliffe did not want to be in her company should the law catch up with him.

"I never got 'round to telling you my name," Mark drawled, not mentioning his thought to Winnie. "It's Mark Counter———"

"Them Wycliffes talked about you," Winnie answered. "Billy claimed when they found out they'd made a mistake and who Sam was that shooting him helped them get evens for what you did to them in some saloon. Is that why Loney Sandel tried to kill you after you saved him?"

"Some of it," Mark replied. "When I saw the dun, I thought maybe the Kaddo got Billy."

"He wasn't with us," the girl said. "Are you after Billy now?"

"After we've put you someplace safe," Mark agreed.

"Don't you bother none about *that*!" Winnie hissed. "You take me along so's I can see that damned Billy get his. He's the worst of them all."

"Maybe as safe to take her on as try to go back," Tejas put in. "Kaddo're behind us."

"How far's this Pegler place?" Mark inquired.

"Not know," admitted Tejas. "But river getting smaller. What you want to do, *amigo*?"

"We may as well keep going. At least, if the worst comes to the worst we can fort up at the trading post."

When agreeing to Mark's going after the Wycliffes, Murat had stated his intention of gathering a strong posse and following should the blond giant not return by the end of the week. If the Kaddo did corner Mark's party at the trading post, they ought to be able to hold out until help arrived.

Receiving the girl's assurance that she could stand up to the journey, Mark and Tejas made preparations to leave. The Indian went ahead as scout and selected a route which kept them from being seen on a skyline, or offered cover in which they might hide to make a fight should the need arise. While they saw no raiding parties, Tejas found tracks which told of considerable Indian movement.

"Hunting parties, maybe," Mark suggested when given the news.

"Indian only hunt buffalo in bunches of ten or more," Tejas replied. "Too many braves make noise, scare off deer. This not buffalo country."

"On the war path then."

"Maybe so. Not have women with them. Could be raiding."

"Is there any difference?" Winnie inquired.

"Some," Mark answered. "A war path means just that, they're looking for a fight. When they're raiding, they're out for loot. Sure they'll fight if they have to, but they'd sooner not take chances. Let's get going, Tejas."

Under such conditions travel must be slow, for they had to pick their way carefully. Nor did they stick to the river, but followed a line parallel to it at a distance of a mile. Once they hid among a clump of white oak and chestnut trees for almost an hour while a band of Kaddo braves ate a meal and rested their horses on a slope a quarter of a mile from them. Night came without Mark's party reaching the trading post, or even seeing anything to tell them how close they might be. So they made camp, waiting until after dark before lighting a fire, and finishing off their food.

Dawn came and they rode on again. Before they had covered more than a few hundred yards, Tejas found tracks of six shod horses going in their direction the previous afternoon. Riding on again, the Indian soon came to a stop. The tracks went up a slope and Tejas signaled his companions to halt while he advanced on foot. After peering cautiously over the slope, he turned and waved.

"Get down, we'll walk up there," Mark ordered, noticing that Tejas remained in cover.

"Trading post over ridge," the Indian announced, slipping back down the slope to meet the others. "What's left of it."

Carefully keeping to cover, Mark joined the Indian and looked down a bush-dotted slope to an open valley floor. Only one building remained standing, the other two log cabins having been reduced to burned-out ruins. Even the corrals and woodpile had been destroyed, but Mark could see no sign of the wagon. The six tracks led down to the remains of Pegler's trading post, yet he failed to locate the horses which had made them.

"We'd best go down and take a look," Mark said.

"Could be trap," Tejas warned.

"Stay here with Winnie and cover me then," ordered Mark. "I'll ride in like I don't expect any trouble."

Leaving the girl and Indian, Mark started down the slope. While he rode as if completely unaware of the possibility of danger, he stayed alert and watched the small cabin's front. Lying at the rear of the burned-out buildings, the cabin had one door and window in the front. At its rear, some thirty feet behind, rose the other side of the valley in a sheer wall.

Every instinct Mark possessed warned him that somebody other than his two companions watched him. Try as he might, he could not locate the watchers. Knowing he could trust the stallion, he fastened his reins to the saddlehorn and let them hang. That left his hands free and he used knee pressure to guide the horse while taking out his makings to roll a smoke.

The door of the cabin opened as Mark reached the foot of the slope. He brought the horse to a halt some thirty yards from the building and studied the two men who came out. They wore range clothes, looked a couple of hard cases, but he did not recognize either of them. Noting the wolf-cautious manner in which they darted glances at the valley sides, he guessed they might have had Indian trouble.

"Howdy," greeted the taller of the pair. "You alone?"

"You could say that," Mark agreed. "What's up?"

"Injuns run off our hosses last night," the shorter man replied. "You seen anything of 'em?"

"Nary a sign," Mark drawled. "I've come down from Brady way. It's been a mighty lonesome ride."

"Come ahead and rest your saddle," offered the taller hard case.

Something in the man's attitude rang a warning alarm for Mark. It may have been the way he eyed the big stallion, or the fact that he did not look the sort to offer hospitality without expecting to see a return for his generosity. Left afoot, faced with the possibility of more trouble with the Kaddos, a fast horse would be mighty tempting. However, Mark continued to act as before and gave no hint of his suspicions. He wanted to get closer before making a move.

Then Mark saw the rifle's barrel poking through the loophole in the cabin's wall. Almost imperceptibly he steered the horse so as to put the two men between him and the rifle. He doubted if the man in the cabin would cut loose until the other two were close enough to grab the stallion.

Suddenly the taller man jerked up his head and stared past Mark at the slope down which the blond giant rode.

"Mark!" yelled Winnie's voice. "They're two of the Wycliffe bunch!"

While the girl acted in good faith, she put Mark in one hell of a spot. On seeing him ride toward the men, she thought that he failed to grasp the danger of the situation. Before Tejas could stop her, she rose and ran into view of the two hard cases and shouted her warning.

At the first word Mark thrust himself sideways out of the saddle. Snarling a curse, the taller man grabbed for his gun and his companion followed his lead. Flame ripped from the rifle in the cabin and Mark heard the bullet split the air where his body had been an instant before. While falling, he fetched out his matched guns. Having been in a similar situation, the blood bay started to swing away from its master and loped off to one side.

When Mark struck the ground, he held a cocked Colt in each hand. The right-hand gun spat once, driving its bullet into the body of the taller hard case an instant before he cleared leather. At almost the same moment Tejas intervened from up the slope. Dirt flew between the shot man and his companion. Realizing that Mark had lied when claiming to be alone, the second man turned and sprinted for the cabin.

Close to where Mark landed, a bush offered concealment and some protection from the rifle in the cabin. He cut loose with a shot from either hand, driving the bullets at the loophole. Fast though he moved, his aim proved good. Splinters flew from the edge of the hole and the rifle jerked at the moment its user squeezed the trigger. Instead of coming at Mark, the bullet flew harmlessly into the air. Before the man could reload, Mark rolled behind the bush and wriggled to more satisfactory shelter at the rear of a rock.

Already the rifle slanted down into line again. Glass shattered and a Winchester appeared through the ruined window. Carefully Mark searched the front of the building and could see no other weapons. Then he turned to see what had happened to his companions. He found that Tejas had pulled the girl back into cover and lay behind a tree lining the Spencer at the cabin.

Satisfied that the other two were in no immediate

danger, Mark gave thought to the problem of what to do next. He did not know which of the Wycliffe gang used the cabin, or how many of them, but aimed to find out. Another important point arose; all day they had seen signs of Indians and one of the parties might be within hearing distance. The sound of shooting would bring them like iron filings to a magnet. When that happened, Mark wanted to have the girl inside the cabin. Out in the open they stood no chance. Yet he knew the men in the building would not allow his party to enter.

Once again Mark studied the cabin and surrounding area. They would have to force an entrance and he sought for the means to do so without taking lead in the process. Twisting around, he signaled his intentions to Tejas and the Indian showed that he understood.

Mark's horse stood some distance away, having come to a halt in a hollow, and was partially hidden from the men in the cabin. Wanting the horse, the Wycliffe men were unlikely to shoot it. However it stopped some distance from Mark's position and to reach it meant crossing open ground. So he put aside thoughts of collecting the stallion and went into action on foot.

CHAPTER THIRTEEN

A Student of a Highland Pastime

RISING swiftly, Mark darted away from his horse in the direction of the next piece of cover. His move took the two men at the front of the cabin by surprise and the bullet which came from the window missed him by several feet. Up the slope Tejas' Spencer cracked a reply, although he achieved nothing. Then Mark made another dash and landed safely behind a large rock. From there he progressed in dives, by running or crawling along on his belly, until he reached a point where neither rifle at the front of the building could line on him.

Unfortunately his intention of approaching from the windowless side of the cabin came to nothing. Before making the attempt, he studied the wall and noted it carried loopholes. At one hole a slight but significant movement caught his eye. Unless he missed his guess, a man waited there ready to throw down on him at his first unwary movement. That ruled out any chance of getting close to the building from his present position.

Thrusting himself from cover, Mark raced toward the rear slope. Confirmation of his suspicions came as a rifle's muzzle stabbed through the loophole. Before its user could take aim, Mark dived once more into shelter. He landed where he could study the rear of the cabin. Some thirty feet separated it from the sheer slope and with nothing behind which even a jackrabbit might hide to give cover during an attack on the rear.

"Pegler's done that on purpose," Mark told himself bitterly. "Maybe I'll have better luck on the other side."

With that he went up the slope, which, at that point rose at a gentler angle than behind the cabin. At the top he found that the thick woodland started again, although Pegler had been doing some timber cutting recently. Along the top, level with where the roof of the cabin showed, a tree trunk rested on two sawhorses. Branches and roots had been cut off, leaving a straight log almost twenty feet long suspended between the two X-shaped frames.

Although Mark glanced at the log, he gave it no thought and moved along the edge of the cliff. Then he saw something black against the roof timbers. Alert for danger, his senses screamed a warning which caused him to leap backward. Not a second too soon either. Flame spurted from the hole and a bullet sang through the air where his body had been a moment before.

"Damn him, that Pegler was one smart *hombre*," Mark growled. "That loophole in the roof's a mighty sneaky ace-in-the-hole."

It seemed that the cabin offered good all-round defense, yet the urgency of entering grew greater by the second. Swinging around, Mark studied the country behind him. He noted that it offered ideal cover for any hostile Kaddo bucks who might want to sneak up on him. So far he saw no hint of danger from that angle. True the woods seemed strangely quiet, but the shooting could account for that.

To study the woods Mark had to look across the sawhorses and their burden. Then his eyes dropped to the log. It would be too short by almost ten feet to be pushed across to the cabin, even if doing so would achieve any purpose. However another possibility sprang to mind.

Back in the War, when he rode in Bushrod Sheldon's cavalry, Mark's company commander had been a Scottish major. Angus Farquharson, younger son of a noble house, retained his love of Scotland and introduced the men under him to a number of traditional Highland pastimes. Even then Mark had been very powerful and under Farquharson's guidance became adept at one particular strength sport. Since joining the floating outfit he kept his hand in and won many a bet for the ranch with his skill at tossing the caber.

Walking across to the thicker end of the log, Mark tentatively lifted it and estimated the weight. Unless he missed his guess, the log weighed over two hundred pounds; heavier than he had yet tossed. Kicking the sawhorse aside, he set the butt of the log on the ground. He then went to the other end and raised it until it stood on its end. Resting the weight on his shoulder, he bent down until he could get his hands underneath the butt. After making sure of the balance, he began to straighten up. The old knack had not deserted him. Taking the strain, he thrust himself forward in the windup run for the throw.

On the other slope Tejas and the girl watched without understanding just what use Mark hoped to make of the log. Then they saw, although neither could barely credit the evidence of their eyes. Sighting his Spencer, Tejas fired at the cabin. He guessed at the loophole in the roof and wanted to distract the occupants if possible.

Forward strode Mark, powerful legs driving his body and the burden it bore on. Then he gave a surging heave and propelled the log up into the air. It was a sight which would have gladdened Major Farquharson's Scottish heart, the way the log turned over in the air. Out it sailed, over the edge of the slope to land on the roof of the cabin. While stoutly made, the roof had not been erected to stand up against the impact of some two hundred and twenty pounds of timber crashing down on it. Realizing his danger, Mark threw himself flat after making the magnificent caber toss. He could not see the result of his throw, but heard the creak of breaking wood as the ridge-pole snapped and the roof caved in, followed by the scream of a man in pain.

A moment before, inside the cabin, Evan Shever, fourth member of Wycliffe's party in the Bigfoot Saloon, had turned from his place at the front. He looked to where the second hard case stood on a cupboard after firing at Mark. The cabin was of only one room and bare of furnishings, probably one of the reasons the Indians did not burn it when they had attacked and wiped out Pegler's assistants: Shever had seen the charred bodies in the burned-out buildings on his arrival.

"You get him?" Shever had asked.

"I don't know. That big jasper's fast."

"Dib's cashed out there. Damn Cousin Churn, why'd he have to leave us three here while he went out again?"

"Like he said, he figured to round up the other boys and see if we could find where Pegler went for the silver," the hard case had answered. "If they hear the shooting, they'll come running."

Silence had fallen for a time and the hard case had watched the top of the slope. He had not seen Mark and had failed to notice the erection of the log. Suddenly a bullet had come through the window and sunk into the dirt floor. Wondering if the man on the slope could see him, the hard case had twisted around.

"What's he doing?"

"I don't kn———!" Shever had begun.

At that point a terrific crash had sounded above

them and the roof had caved in. The hard case had
seen his danger a moment too late. Down came the
roof timbers and log, pinning and crushing him under them. Letting out a scream of agony, he stared
wildly across the cabin at Shever.

No help came from that source. Panic filled Shever
as he saw the wreck of the roof and realized that he
no longer had the backing of his two companions.
Thoughts ripped through his head, working at a way
to save himself. After the muscular effort required to
hurl the log on to the cabin, Mark Counter ought to
be so exhausted that he would be temporarily out of
the game. That left the other man, armed with a
Spencer carbine—not the most accurate weapon—
unless Shever missed his guess. At that range Shever
figured he could chance running the gauntlet of the
other's fire in an attempt to reach Mark's blood bay.

Dropping the rifle, and ignoring his companion's
moans for help, Shever jerked open the cabin door.
He sprang out, drawing his right-hand Freeman
revolver, and ran toward the horse. The Spencer
boomed out and its bullet whapped through the air
close to him but he never broke stride or bothered to
shoot back.

Growling a cowhand curse, Tejas lay down his carbine. He had just fired his seventh shot and saw there
would not be time to reload. Nor could he hope to
make a hit at that range with his newly acquired
Cooper revolvers. Telling the girl to keep down, he
thrust himself out of cover and bounded forward.

Shever saw the Indian coming but still made no attempt to use his gun. Instead he concentrated on running as fast as he could to the horse. Holding the
cocked revolver, he started down into the shallow
hollow where the stallion stood. It showed no great
concern at the man's approach, and he felt sure
escape lay close at hand.

From along to the right of the valley a rifle

crashed. Caught in the head by a bullet, Shever pitched forward. His revolver went off, its muzzle-blast singeing the horse's hair and the lead slicing a graze on its rump. Even as the stallion screamed with pain and reared, Shever's body collided with it. Blood and brains smeared the saddle as he slid to the ground and the stallion started running.

Bounding down the slope, Tejas heard the shot and twisted around. Two Kaddo braves knelt in sight behind bushes and three more came into view from various points of concealment. Smoke rose from the Springfield rifle cradled against one of the pair's shoulder. The other lined a Sharps carbine at Tejas. Before the young Indian could make a move to save himself, flame licked from the Sharp's barrel. He felt the shocking impact of the heavy bullet, spun around and fell to the ground. Badly wounded, he still tried to raise his revolver as the braves ran toward him. Halting, a buck whipped up and drew back his bow. The arrow flashed forward and completed the work the bullet began.

Up on the slope Winnie saw Tejas die and the Kaddo braves leaping toward him. So intent on counting coup and collecting loot were they that none gave the girl a thought. Unlike when she gave her warning to Mark, Winnie remained in hiding. She realized that showing herself would be asking for a painful death.

While young, poorly educated and filled with romantic notions, Winnie possessed a fair share of good Texas common sense. Being unarmed, she could do nothing for her companions. Instinctively she knew what Mark would want her to do. So she put aside any thoughts of staying around and slipped back. When sure that the braves could not see her, she rose and ran to the waiting horses. Unfastening the dun, she swung astride it and started it running.

At first the girl rode with the fear of pursuit filling

her. Then the feeling left her and good sense caused her to draw rein. During the time she rode with Mark and Tejas, Winnie learned some lessons. So she found a place where she and the horse could hide before halting. Studying her back trail, she concluded that nobody followed her. Then she gave thought to what she should do for the best.

"We come up river," she told herself. "So if I can find it and ride down, I ought to reach some settler's place—if the Injuns don't get me first."

With that the girl started the dun moving. She rode at a trot, scanning the country ahead of her regularly and often turning to look back along her tracks. Seeing birds rising from the trees ahead of her, she decided to take cover until finding what had alarmed them. Hiding among some bushes, she retained sufficient presence of mind to keep the dun quiet. That proved fortunate for a party of Kaddo braves rode by, heading toward the trading post. Watching them go, she saw puffs of smoke rise into the air. However she lacked the skill to know that the smoke signals originated from some place beyond the post.

Although the Indians rode straight by, Winnie did not offer to leave her hiding place for almost an hour. Deciding at last that she could ride on in safety, she started the dun moving in what she hoped would be the right direction. Time passed, although she had no way of judging it in hours and minutes, until an uneasy feeling came to her. Slowly she began to wonder if she had picked the right direction, she wondered if the Pedernales River did lie ahead of her.

Coming to a small stream, she halted the horse and allowed it to drink. As she slipped from the saddle, her eyes went to the water. For a moment the significance of what she saw did not sink in. Then she realized that the steam flowed in the opposite direction to which she had been riding. Her instincts told her that the stream joined the Pedernales and she must retrace her route. By following the stream, she would find the river.

By that time the sun hung low in the western sky. No child, even a girl, grew up on a small spread in frontier-Texas without learning how to live off the country. So the desire to survive forced Winnie to look for food. She gathered edible fruit and nuts while looking for a safe place to spend the night. They would fill her stomach and keep her going until she could find more appetizing food.

Finding a small valley close to the stream, she prepared to spend the night in it. First she cared for the horse, off-saddling it and making sure that she fastened it securely to a small tree. The dun offered her only small chance of survival and she did not dare take the chance of being left afoot. Although the Kaddos had taken Sandel's bed roll as part of their loot. Mark had fastened the blanket Winnie used to the dun's saddle. So she could make use of it to give some protection and warmth during the night.

After the dreary, restless hours of darkness dragged away, Winnie rose cold and stiff in the light of the early morning. In one respect she could thank the Kaddo; their roaming bands scared off most of the larger wild life, including bears, cougar or wolves, all of which possessed a taste for horse flesh. Saddling the dun took time and she did not dare ride at any speed. Nor could she if she hoped to following the windings of the small stream. She decided against leaving the water for fear of again losing her direction.

Noon came and went without a sight of the river. Just as despair began to fill the girl, she saw water glinting through the trees ahead. More water than ran in the little stream. Feeling almost like crying with relief, she came on to the bank of the Pedernales River. Once again she decided to ride by the water, taking her chance on running into more Indians rather than risk losing her way.

Holding her horse to a steady trot, which slowed to a walk as the sun rose toward its noon height, Winnie followed the flow of the river. She saw no sign of human beings of any kind and slowly started to lose her fear. An animal track led through sassafrass bushes and she rode along it with more confidence than she had felt since beginning her flight at Pegler's trading post.

Suddenly a man lunged up from among the bushes, catching hold of the dun's reigns and bringing it to a halt. Even as Winnie opened her mouth to scream, she realized that he was no Indian. Tall, well-built, young looking despite a beard, clad in range clothes and belting two Army Colts, she recognized him as one of Wycliffe's men. More than that, he had been the one Churn Wycliffe treated as an equal—and accompanied Billy when the party split up.

"Just look who's here, will you," said Billy's voice from the other side of the trail. "It looks like she done snuck off from Loney, and with my hoss."

"There's more to it than that, from the look of her," replied the bearded man as his companions came into sight. "Where's Loney and the boys, gal?"

"Got killed by the Injuns," Winnie answered.

"How'd you get away?" Billy demanded, slouching up with a stocky hard case on his heels.

"Mark Counter and an Indian called Tejas saved me."

"Where're they now?" the bearded man, Augie by name, snapped.

"At Pegler's trading post. There were more Injuns there," Winnie replied.

"Any of our boys there?" Augie wanted to know, although the other two showed more interest in the girl's back trail than for their companions' welfare.

"Th—Three of them," the girl told him.

"Uncle Churn?"

"Not that I know of. It was the other one———"

"Cousin Evan," Billy growled. "They get him?"

"They got all of them, Mark, the Indian—I got to my hoss and ran."

"When was this, gal?" Augie inquired gently.

"Yesterday. I've been riding and hiding ever since."

"See any Injuns?"

"Only one bunch. They went riding toward the trading post."

"That bunch we saw were headed upriver," commented the hard case.

"Sure did, Rags," Augie agreed. "Took with the smoke we saw going up, it could be their chiefs're calling them in to the camp."

"What're we going to do?" Rags inquired and it was significant that he turned to Augie for advice.

"Go to the trading post and see if Churn's made it there," Augie answered.

"I say we head down the river," Billy put in.

"How about Churn and the other boys?" Augie growled.

"The gal said they're all cashed———"

"Only Loney and Evan's bunches," Augie pointed out. "If Churn's alive, he's likely headed for the post. Six guns stand a better chance than three."

"I've thought all along this was a damned fool game!" Billy spat out. "Now I say we get the hell back toward Lake Travis and head for home."

"Nobody's stopping you going, Billy boy," Augie replied. "Just turn your hoss and ride."

"How about you, Rags?" Billy asked.

"I'm with Augie."

"It's your scalp. Me 'n' the gal———"

"The gal stays with us," interrupted Augie. "You do what you want."

Only for a moment did anger show on Billy's face. Then he made an effort and regained control of himself. Although his uncle gave him nominal command of the trio, Augie had taken over as their leader almost from leaving the rest of the band. Nor had Billy objected, for the bearded man's guidance had kept them safe despite the fact that they saw plenty of Indian sign. Billy figured himself to be good with a gun, but knew Augie to be better. So he accepted the other's quiet-spoken order with as good grace as he could manage.

"All right, already," he said. "I'll go along with you."

"Take the point, Rags," Augie ordered. "Ride careful and if you see anything at all get back here *pronto.*"

"Sure, Augie," Rags replied and disappeared into the bushes.

"You ride ahead of me and the girl, Billy," the bearded man went on.

"Yeah!" grunted the young man.

Collecting their horses, the three men started to put Augie's orders into operation. Tired, frightened, hungry, Winnie kept her horse at the bearded man's side and prayed that they might meet up with Churn Wycliffe's party before reaching the trading post.

"Rags's coming!" Billy hissed, twisting around in his saddle.

Galloping up, Rags slid his horse to a halt before reaching the others. He signaled and Augie told the girl to dismount. Then he left Billy to watch her and joined the other man. Whatever news Rags brought, he clearly did not want the girl to hear it. Dropping his voice to a whisper, he passed on his information to Augie.

"Are you sure?" the bearded man snapped.

"I didn't stick around long, but I'm sure enough."

"What's up?" Billy called worriedly.

"Get your rifle and bring mine," Augie answered. "Rags, stick by the gal and keep her quiet."

CHAPTER FOURTEEN

A Primitive Piece of Mining Equipment

AFTER the exertion of making the tremendous throw with the log, Mark had stayed on the ground. He wanted a few seconds to recover from his great effort, knowing the need to be fully alert before tangling in a gun fight. Hearing the shooting, he thrust himself erect in time to see Shever killed and his horse go racing off out of the valley. Even as the situation sank home and he started forward, sounds behind him gave a grim warning. Before he could turn to investigate, something hissed through the air. The loop of a hair rope dropped over his head, tightened about his upper arms, then jerked him backward.

With an effort Mark caught his balance and twisted around, his arms forcing against the constriction of the rope. Several Kaddo bucks rushed at him and, to his surprise, they came without weapons in their hands. A brawny buck gripped the rope which trapped Mark's arms, leaning back in his attempt to maintain the loop's grip. Mark threw his weight backward, jerking the rope-wielder toward him. In the background stood a war bonnet chief with a Winchester rifle cradled across his arm. He yelled something to the braves, but made no attempt to use the weapon.

Having gained some slack on the loop, Mark stabbed his hands toward the Colts' butts. Deftly

the brave holding the rope halted his forward progress, flexing and snapping back with his arms. Just
as Mark's hands closed on the ivory handles, the
rope's loop tightened. While loose it slipped lower
and gripped just below the elbows, effectively preventing him from drawing the Colts. Showing a skill
equal to any cowhand, the Kaddo flicked the rope to
send a coil snaking along it. Although Mark knew
what the brave intended, he could not counter the
move. Twirling over his head, the coil tightened
about his upper arms and added to the grip of the
loop.

Screeching in triumph, the rest of the braves
descended on Mark. They flung themselves at the
blond giant and bore him to the ground. Hands
closed upon his body, others wrenched the Colts
from their holsters. Knowing the penalty for being
taken alive by hostile Indians, Mark put up a tremendous struggle. Two braves went flying, thrown
through the air by his powerful legs, but not even the
big Texan's strength could prevail against such odds.
With his arms free he might have done more, but the
two turns of rope held fast. At last sheer weight of
numbers wore him down. The Kaddo worked fast,
securing his ankles and wrists with knots that would
not slip.

Bound and helpless, Mark watched the Kaddo
chief walk in his direction. The braves drew back and
their leader gave orders to them. Some of the party
turned and faded off into the woods from which they
had stalked to capture him.

"Will you ride, big one, or be thrown across the
back of a horse?" asked the chief in Spanish.

"I'll ride," Mark answered.

Sitting astride a horse there might be a slight
chance of escape. Certainly riding offered a greater
opportunity than being taken along slung bodily over
a saddle. Mark wondered a little at the cause of the
offer, also why the Indians went to the trouble of

taking him alive. He could guess what happened. Most probably the Kaddo left scouts to watch the cabin, with the main body waiting close by ready to strike at the most favorable moment. Seeing Mark's arrival, the scouts alerted their chief and he gave orders which sent braves moving in silence to grab any advantage offered to them.

After checking on the ropes holding his arms, the braves freed Mark's ankles and helped him to his feet. Turning, he looked across the valley to learn what had happened to his friends. Already scalping knives had done their work and loot from the bodies had been gathered. A brave, carrying Tejas' Spencer and the Cooper-loaded gunbelt, came up the slope and approached the chief. Although unable to follow the conversation, Mark guessed from various gestures at its meaning. He decided that the brave mentioned Winnie and asked what they should do about her. Looking at the top of the other slope, Mark saw two braves appear leading Tejas' horse. From all signs the girl must have fled and the brave wanted to know whether they should take out after her. With something like relief Mark watched the chief shake his head, rattle out a few words and point to the west.

"Your woman has run away, big one," the chief told Mark.

"Are you fixing to follow her?" asked Mark.

"No. By the time my men bring horses she will be far away. There are more of our warriors down the river. If they do not find her, she will die in the woods."

"And what of me?"

"You are coming to our place of medicine."

Which left a whole heap unexplained and gave Mark food for conjecture. He could guess at the reason for taking him with them now they had him prisoner, but still felt puzzled at their actions. Like all Indians, the Kaddo tortured prisoners but Mark had never heard of them going out of their way to capture men to do it. Just about the only consolation left was that Winnie appeared to have made good her escape. Given just one mite of luck the girl ought to reach the Pedernales River and follow it down to safety.

A faint grin creased Mark's face as he saw the mount selected to carry him. Although it carried a saddle, the boney scrub possessed none of the qualities he normally expected in a riding horse. With that sorry bang-tail between his knees he could not hope to outride his captors, which, as he well knew, was why they put him on it. Being a smart fighting man, Mark understood when he must sit back and do nothing. As long as life remained, there was hope. He did not doubt that the Kaddos would kill him if he made trouble for them.

Pushing their horses hard, the Indians led Mark to the west. They passed through wooded land and along rocky valleys, winding their way along with complete assurance through what seemed almost like a maze to their prisoner. At last they turned into the mouth of a canyon. Passing around a corner Mark found they had arrived at their destination.

Tepees scattered in an untidy circle across the floor of the canyon, which appeared to be blind, having its further end closed by a rock wall. Although a few young women appeared from the tepees, Mark saw that most of the camp's occupants were men of warrior age.

"Get down," ordered the chief, halting the party before one of the largest tepees and looking at Mark.

A man stepped from inside the tepee. Although he wore the dress of a Kaddo chief, he had a white man's face, especially about the cheeks and lips. While the chief spoke in rapid Kaddo, Mark studied the white man and a suspicion arose. Mark could guess that he was the subject of the conversation for both chief and white man directed long glances in his direction. It seemed that the chief told of how Mark threw the log on to the cabin, for he went through the motions of bending, raising and heaving something heavy and used his hands to indicate the bulk of the object.

"Bear Killer here tells me you're a real mighty man, feller," the white man finally remarked, turning to Mark.

"You could say that, Mr. Pegler," the blond giant answered, putting his theory to the test.

Surprise etched itself on the man's face and Mark knew that his guess at the other's identity proved correct.

"You're smarter than the other one," Pegler growled. "Him and me've played poker in the same game a couple of times and he didn't recognize me. Only I don't even remember ever meeting you afore."

"You never did," Mark admitted. "I heard you wore a bushy beard. Your face hasn't tanned since you shaved it off."

"Smart thinking. Is that why Churn Wycliffe brought you along?"

"Nope."

"You're working with ole Churn to find my silver mine though, aren't you?"

"Nope," repeated Mark. "I came after him and his bunch."

"Now why'd anybody want to come after a mean bunch like them?" Pegler asked, for the word "after" used in such a manner meant only one thing, hunting down the other party for some serious purpose. "Light down from that saddle and rest your butt end. I'd say you're used to something better in hoss flesh than that crow-bait they gave you."

"You never said a truer word," Mark replied sincerely, tossing his right leg across the saddle and dropping to the ground. "I wouldn't wish even a Kansas fighting-pimp* to have to ride that horse."

* Fighting-pimp: Texans' derogatory name for Kansas peace officers.

"You fixing to tell me what brought you after the Wycliffes?" Pegler asked.

"Billy killed an old pard of mine and I figured on asking why. Only I didn't count on running into Indian fuss like this."

"Just one man and you figured to take on the Wycliffe bunch?"

"There were two of us; your bucks killed the other at the trading post."

Before any more could be said, the chief spoke and pointed along the canyon. Following the other men's gaze, Mark saw a strange sight. A wide ledge around eight feet high ran the length of the end wall, with a set of steps carved up from the ground at one end. Roughly in the center of the ledge a slot maybe four feet wide and three deep had been cut—it formed too perfect a rectangle to be entirely natural—into the rock. Above the slot stood what looked like an exceptionally strong and powerful windlass for a well, with handles on either end of the spindle. The rope around the spindle was of greater strength than ever seen on a well; and needed to be, for its end appeared to be connected to the top of a block of rock which stood on the ledge and had been shaped to pass up and down the slot.

"You find it interesting?" Pegler asked.

"I might if I knew what the hell it was," Mark replied.

"It's a primitive piece of mining equipment. I'd bet you've never seen its like before."

"You'd win."

"Few people would know its purpose," Pegler grinned and his voice took on the tone of an educated man. "In fact it wasn't until I saw the raw silver Bear Killer brought in to trade that I realized what it was."

"Feel like telling me?" Mark asked.

"It's a press for crushing the ore-bearing rock. I rigged it up again in the hope of——Say, you know me, but I don't know you."

"Matt—Smith," Mark answered.

"Is that your summer name?"

"It does well enough any time."

"Come on into my tepee, you look like you could take a meal."

"Won't the Injuns object?" Mark asked.

"Not as long as you don't try any fool stunts," Pegler replied and spoke to the chief. At first Bear Killer seemed inclined to object, but finally grunted and walked away. Pegler grinned at Mark, "Go on inside."

"How about cutting me free?"

"Sure. Only don't try anything stupid like making a run for it. I've got an offer for you if you're interested."

"I'm interested in anything that'll keep me alive," Mark admitted frankly.

"Play along with me and you'll not only be kept alive, I'll make you rich too," Pegler promised, taking the knife from his belt sheath and cutting the ropes which bound the blond giant's arms.

Mark looked at Pegler with interest as the ropes fell away. Clearly the man had some hold over the Indians, for none raised any objections to his actions'. Further proof came with the arrival of bowls of hot, nourishing stew. While Mark ate, Pegler left the tepee to return carrying the blond giant's gunbelt with its Colts in the holsters. However, Pegler placed them at the far side of the tepee.

"They've no caps on and the loads've been drawn," the trader warned. "Later I'll see you're given powder and shot."

"How're you going to make me rich?" Mark asked. "And why?"

"Why's easy. I'm going to need a good man backing me in the future."

"And I'm a good man?"

"Anybody who goes hunting the Wycliffes for evens is either *loco*, or tough and real good with a gun. You're not *loco*. From what I've heard, you're strong and tough. That gunbelt tells me you're good with a gun."

"I can take 'em out fast enough when I have to," Mark admitted. "And hit what I aim at as long as it's not too far off. You want for me to show you?"

"Later maybe," grinned Pegler. "When I'm sure I can trust you. I reckon I'll have a better chance of doing that when I've told you some about me."

"Go right ahead and tell me," offered Mark. "I've nothing but time right now."

Although Pegler did not go into details, he hinted that he came to Texas on the run from the law. A trained engineer, he did not dare to chance following his profession even in frontier Texas. However he possessed enough money to set up as a trader. Seeking an area where he would not come into too great contact with other white men, he settled on the head waters of the Pedernales. At that time the Kaddos maintained an uneasy peace with the white brother and his business grew steadily.

Then Bear Killer brought in some raw silver to trade—and knew something of its value. The chief refused to take anything but a repeating rifle and ammunition for the silver and hinted that he could bring in more to buy other weapons. However he declined to disclose the source of the silver and warned against any attempts to find it.

"Most folks'd've gone ahead and looked, either getting killed or turning the Injuns against them," Pegler stated smugly. "But not me. No, sir. I traded guns for silver and added a few jugs of whisky when asked. Guns and bullets were the main thing. I didn't want the Kaddos getting liquored up and starting a scalphunt—at least not until I was ready for it."

"You wanted to have time to light out before they began?" Mark suggested.

"Something like that."

From the mocking grin on Pegler's face, Mark

guessed a deeper motive was involved. As Pegler
clearly wanted to tell the story in his own way, Mark
refrained from asking questions. He eyed the trader
up and down. Something over middle height,
brawny, he would still be no more than child's play
for the blond giant to handle when a chance arose.
Until then Mark aimed to learn all he could and keep
Pegler believing in his support for whatever the
trader planned.

Continuing his story, Pegler told how he gained
the chief's confidence and became accepted by the
tribe. With the aid of chloroform and other scientific
wonders the Indians had never seen, backed by pre-
dictions of carefully arranged accidents, he won the
reputation of a medicine man. Backed by his new
found position, he demanded to be shown where the
silver originated. Unwilling to go against popular
opinion, Bear Killer brought Pegler to the canyon
and showed him the hidden entrance of a cave. Inside
Pegler found many sacks holding the raw silver and a
sizeable stack of rocks bearing veins of the precious
material. Seeing and recognizing the primitive press,
he rebuilt the windlass and prepared to start mining
operations.

At which point he discovered that the original
miners—Spanish explorers from the days before
Texas gained her independence—suffered a cave-in
which fetched down all their workings.

"There's a fortune in silver to be brought out,"
Pegler informed Mark. "But the Kaddo won't let me
mine it. This's a medicine place; they wiped out the
greaser miners for digging here. It was all I could do
to get them to let me work the rock from the cave.
One thing they won't do is give me permission to
bring in the modern equipment to get the mine
working again."

"There went my fortune," Mark said dryly.

"Maybe not," Pegler replied. "I still plan to mine
that silver."

"With me holding off the Kaddo while you do it?" Mark scoffed. "Mister, are you sure you didn't reckon I was crazy enough, not tough or fast enough to go after the Wycliffes?"

"Nope. When we come here to start mining, there won't be any trouble from the Kaddos."

"Just how do you figure that out?"

"The U.S. Army'll have tended to them for us."

"Why should they?" Mark demanded. "The Kaddo're reasonably peaceable and nobody wants this neck of the woods bad enough to come after it."

"I've spent time priming the Kaddos for trouble," Pegler said quietly. "One of the reasons they kept the peace was because they wanted guns before starting to make war. Another was that they figured no white folks wanted their land. Now they've got the guns—and figure somebody's after the land."

"Meaning Wycliffe and his bunch?"

"Meaning Wycliffe and his bunch. One of my men brought me word that they'd learned about the silver and were coming after it. A stinking pedlar found out and sold the news to Churn Wycliffe. My man stayed long enough to learn what Wycliffe planned and then high-tailed it to me with the word. So I reckoned the time had finally come for me to kill off Joe Pegler."

"You burned your own place down?" Mark said.

"What better way to make sure that nobody could identify the bodies?" the trader asked. "I had a couple of half-breed helpers and a pair of white trash. Between them they'd been robbing me blind for years. So I figured I might as well make them pay for it and be more use to me dead than they ever were alive. I couldn't leave them alive and talking; and they'd've been nothing but trouble if I fetched them along."

Hooves drummed outside and the two men rose to look through the door. A party of braves rode into the camp area, heading for the chief's tepee.

"Who're they?" Mark asked.

"Scouting parties. Bear Killer must've called them in."

"Why'd your men be trouble had you brought them here?"

"One of their pards, a breed, used to come with me, but he laid hands on a Kaddo girl. I thought I was a goner then. The chief figured to hang the breed head down over a fire, only I showed him a better way. It was just after we'd rebuilt the windlass. I put the breed in the slot and we lowered that big block of granite down on to him. He held it off for nearly a minute before it got him. The sight satisfied the braves and kept them off me."

"So you figure to start the Kaddo on the warpath, then the cavalry'll be sent to wipe them out, or shove them on to a reservation?"

"Sure. Then we'll come here, having already taken out the mineral rights to this area. I'm not good with a gun, that's why I want somebody like you backing me."

Fury rose inside Mark as he looked at the trader. Even as he tensed to hurl himself at Pegler and finish the man with his bare hands, Mark heard a considerable commotion outside the tepee. Once again they went to the door, seeing Bear Killer and an elderly man approaching. From the excellent quality of his clothing, the designs on it and the buffalo skull headdress worn by the chief's companion, Mark decided he must be a senior medicine man of the tribe. A moment later Pegler confirmed the conclusion.

"Damnit!" the trader snorted. "That's Moon Watcher. He was their boss medicine man afore I took over and hates my guts. What in hell does he want here?"

Coming to a halt, Bear Killer spoke to Pegler and Mark could see that the words did not please the trader.

"What's up?" Mark inquired.

"Seems that some bucks were killed last night and they figure to take the warpath," Pegler answered. "Only that old bastard, Moon Watcher wants a sign that the Great Spirit favors war."

At that moment a group of braves appeared from a tepee dragging Churn Wycliffe between them. He looked in poor shape, half naked, hair and beard matted with blood, one arm crudely bandaged and a raw gash showed through a tear in his right trouser leg. Making nothing of Wycliffe's feeble attempts to struggle, the braves dragged him to the end wall and thrust him into the slot. Looking at the windlass, Mark saw four braves standing at the handles and the block of granite hung over the slot's mouth.

"What the hell?" Mark growled.

"Moon Watcher asked for a sign, we're going to give him one," Pegler replied. "When we put a feller under that block one time I told the Kaddos that they'd crush the white men like the rock crushed him. Bear Killer allows that Wycliffe's a real strong feller and he's putting him to the test. They'll lower the block down easy. If Wycliffe can save himself, they'll call off the war——Fact being, that's why Bear Killer had you took alive, figured you'd give his boys some more sport. I warned him that you just might spoil his medicine, so he handed you over to me to soften up for later. Come on, this's always worth watching."

CHAPTER FIFTEEN

A Slender Chance to Keep the Peace

MARK and Pegler walked forward, mingling with the Indians who stood before the canyon wall. Already the block started to sink down, the braves at the windlass strained against the drag it imposed upon the spindle. Crouched in the slot, Wycliffe suddenly became aware of the interest showed by the crowd. Looking up, he saw the block. A low moan of terror broke from his lips and he tried to move out of the slot. Standing ready to deal with such an action, two braves used their lances' points to drive him back again.

Sucking in a deep breath, Mark thought of things the Ysabel Kid told him about Indians. One thing all the fighting tribes had in common was their belief in good and bad medicine. When making ready for war they consulted the medicine men and asked for guidance, preferably a sign that the Great Spirit favored their line of action. Let anything happen to spoil their chosen medicine and they would not go out to fight.

All too well Mark knew the horrors of an Indian war. Sure the U.S. Army possessed the weapons to whip the Kaddo, but first many white folk would die. After the Kaddo being so long at peace, the settlers around their country were unlikely to expect trouble. Unless something could be done to stop it, there would be murder, arson and looting—and a tribe of

Indians, poor dupes of an evil white man, most likely wiped off the face of the earth.

Only one thing could stop it happening, for the Kaddo's medicine to be broken. Mark knew the only way that could be done and aimed to make a try at doing it.

Before Pegler realized what he planned, Mark lunged forward. He went through the crowd like it did not exist, sprang forward to brush aside the lance-armed guards and went toward the slot. Shooting out his right hand, Mark caught Wycliffe by the neck and heaved him from beneath the rock. A low rumble of anger rolled from the crowd, then died as they realized that Mark did not merely save the other white man from being crushed.

Turning, Mark backed into the slot. He bent his legs slightly, bowed his head forward and let the weight settle on his shoulders. Slowly and carefully he moved up his hands, placing the flat of his palms against the rough bottom of the block, then bracing himself. The meal and rest in Pegler's tepee had given him a chance to regain his full power and he knew that he was going to need every ounce of strength in the minutes ahead.

Excited comments rose from the watching crowd. The braves at the windlass left the handles and moved to the edge of the ledge to see what happened. Giving a low snarl of rage, Pegler started to move forward. He guessed what Mark planned and fury filled him at what he regarded as the blond giant's treachery. A powerful hand closed on the trader's arm and halted him. Turning, Pegler looked into the cold eyes of the chief.

"Leave him, Hair Face!" Bear Killer ordered. "If your medicine is good, it cannot fail."

Something told Pegler that he had better not force the issue. Then he gave a shrug. Although he did not mention the fact to Mark, the block had been used to crush men more than once. After the first demonstration the Kaddo used it on their own law-breakers or other Indians who fell into their hands. No man ever survived the crushing weight of the block. With the big man dead, the Kaddo would take to the warpath and Pegler ought to be able to slip away in the confusion. Skilled fighting men had never been in such short supply in Texas that he could not hire other help to push through his plans.

After stopping the rock's downward movement, Mark studied the situation and made a shocking discovery. It had been his intention to tip the rock forward from the slot and found it to be impossible. The old Spanish miners knew their work. To prevent accidents they cut the slot narrower at the front than against the wall and carved the block accordingly. So it could not be turned out at the front and must go back through the top.

That left only one way out of the problem.

Slowly Mark started to thrust upward with his hands and shoulders while his powerful leg muscles fought to straighten him up. At first nothing happened; the block remaining exactly where it had been when the braves released the windlass handles. Then slowly, so slowly at first that even the eagle-eyed Bear Killer failed to detect the movement, the mass of granite began to rise. Mark's legs straightened, bracing apart on the rocky ground. Gradually the weight on his shoulders eased but it grew upon his arms.

Much as he wanted, Mark knew he must not stop his attempt at lifting. If the weight sank down he could never raise it again. Before his eyes swam a picture of blazing cabins, screaming women and children being killed, all the horrors that would be turned loose should he fail. He could not hear the excited chatter of the braves as they watched that great block of granite slowly move upward.

Pegler's eyes bulged in disbelief as he watched the darker mass of the block show above the level of the ledge. First an inch showed, then two, three and more. The trader realized what Mark's actions meant. If the blond giant lifted the block back on to the ledge, the Kaddo would consider their medicine bad. Even now only the young, hot-headed bucks called for war. Older, wiser heads debated long, with many calls to follow the Comanche's lead in making a permanent peace. Given the sight of their prime war medicine broken, those who sought peace could present an argument even the most hotheaded buck would understand.

That could not be allowed to happen. With a fortune in silver waiting, nothing must happen to ruin Pegler's plans.

Forcing himself to act calmly and walk with a nonchalant air, Pegler stepped away from Bear Killer. Then he made his way toward the wall, eyes on Mark all the time. Already the block stood well over halfway out of the slot. Strain contorted Mark's face and his muscular frame quivered in its giant effort. If anything happened to ruin his concentration, the granite would crush him to the ground. With that thought in mind, Pegler slid the knife from his belt sheath. He held it so the Indians could not see the blade in his hand.

Mark saw the knife and understood its purpose. Gathering himself, he put every last ounce of strength he possessed into a final surging thrust. Up shot the block, tilting forward at the top of the slot. For a moment it hung motionless and then the weight dragged it over. Mark felt the pressure leaving his arms and heard the wild shouts of the crowd.

Knife held for a belly-ripping slash, Pegler lunged toward the slot. Then he sensed rather than saw the black mass tumbling toward him. Maybe if he had continued forward he might have saved himself. Instead he dug in his front foot and tried to throw his body back to safety. Down came the block, four hundred pounds of granite, on to Pegler. He screamed

once, then bones crashed and blood burst from rup-
tured flesh as the block squashed him into the ground.

Weak with exhaustion Mark fell against the back
of the slot. Though sweat half blinded him, he saw
and heard enough to tell him what happened to
Pegler. Much as he felt the man deserved to die,
Mark pitied him and nausea rose at the sight of what
lay under the block.

The sight caused even the Indians to draw back
and stare with horror-filled eyes. Before any of them
recovered, hooves drummed loud, coming along the
canyon.

A huge white stallion thundered up. Seated on it
was a tall, lean man who wore only a blue breechclout and moccasins, with a gunbelt supporting a
Dragoon Colt at one side and bowie knife on the
other about his waist. Maybe he had shorter hair
than any Indian brave, but he carried a war lance in
his right hand and his face bore the savage lines of a
warrior on the rampage.

Bringing his stallion to a rump-sliding halt, the
rider landed on his feet between Mark and the Kaddo. Amazement showed on their faces as they stared
at the apparition and superstitious awe rose in every
breast for none could think from where the
newcomer sprang.

On backtracking Mark's stallion, the Ysabel Kid
had read the story of its flight and finally reached the
trading post. Again the sign told him all he needed to
know, that his *amigo* had been taken a prisoner by
the Kaddo. Then the Kid stopped being a white man
and turned into that most deadly of fighting
machines, a Comanche Dog Soldier.

Although he traveled light, he carried, as always, a
pair of moccasins and the breechclout of his mother's
people. Stripping off his white man's clothing, he
donned the dress of a *Pehnane* who rode to war
Pukutsi—and when a *Pehnane* rode that way he
aimed to raise all hell and shove a chuck under it.

Dressed and armed in a fitting manner, with his other clothes bundled on the blood bay's saddle, he set off to rescue the blond giant or die in the attempt. When a *Pehnane* went *Pukutsi* there were no half measures; he could only succeed or be killed to stop him.

To a man of the Kid's ability there was no difficulty in following the tracks of Mark's captors. Even when it became too dark for him to read sign, his ears showed him the way.

On arrival at the canyon, the Kid saw Mark take Wycliffe's place under the block and guessed what might be happening. Before leaving his grandfather's new camp, the Kid heard a medicine woman tell of the unrest among the Kaddo. How she knew, he could not imagine, but she claimed the other tribe believed they possessed medicine to crush the white men. If Mark knew of that, he might be trying to break the medicine.

Another alternative came to mind. Occasionally Indians would give a prisoner they admired a trial of strength or courage by which he could win his freedom. In such trials the chances of success were negligible, but the Kid knew better than interfere. To charge down in a do-or-die rescue attempt might distract Mark, cause him to weaken his hold and bring the rock upon him. So the Kid sat and watched, amazed despite his knowledge of Mark's great strength. From his place the Kid could not see Pegler clearly enough to recognize the danger. Before he realized what the trader intended, the rock fell and saved him from further concern on that score. Setting his horse running, he charged down to make sure that Mark received his winner's due.

"Who are you?" demanded Moon Watcher, first to recover from his surprise at the Kid's appearance.

"My people call me *Cuchilo*, the Knife."

"Who are your people?" the medicine man inquired.

Releasing his hold of the lance with his right hand,

the Kid turned it palm downwards. With his forearm bent before his chest, he moved it to the right in a wriggling motion.

"The Snake Going Backward!" breathed Moon Watcher.

"I am of the *Nemenuh*," agreed the Kid.

"The Enemy People," said Bear Killer, nodding in acceptance.

Three names, but they all meant one thing—Comanche. The tribal sign came from an old Comanche legend.* No matter to which band he belonged, any Comanche said he was *Nemenuh*, one of *the* People. To all other tribes the last name proved most correct. Even those tribes, like the Kaddo, who occasionally lived at peace with the Comanche used the name *Tshaoh*, the Enemy People.

While the older men present showed signs of being impressed, a couple of young bucks let out derisive laughs. Fresh from their first war trail, each showed signs of successful encounters. One wore Sandel's gunbelt with the Coopers in the holsters, although the bow he used to deliver the *coup de grace* to Tejas had been left in his tepee. The other cradled Tejas' Spencer carbine on the crook of his arm and a scalp of long Indian-black hair dangled from his belt.

"The *Tshaoh* used to be fighting men," jeered the buck with the Spencer. "But no more."

"Now they are like old squaws," his companion went on. "Begging for food and shelter from the white m———"

The first part of the conversation had been in Spanish, a language most Texas Indians understood. While the Kid spoke some Kaddo, he wanted Mark to be able to follow what was said. Hearing the mocking words, the Kid acted as would any Comanche *tehnap*† when insulted by a youngster barely beyond the horse-herding age.

* Told in *Comanche*.

† *Tehnap:* an experienced warrior.

Pivoting smoothly around, he drove the butt of the lance shaft up and on to the jaw of the buck with the Spencer. In continuation of the move, as the buck reeled backward and dropped his weapon, the Kid met the other's challenge. One glance told him that he did not need to worry even though the second buck grabbed for the Coopers. Before either revolver cleared leather, the end of the lance rammed with some force into the buck's belly. A strangled croak broke from him and he doubled over with hands clawing to his middle instead of continuing to draw the guns. With the lance still gripped in both hands, the Kid swung it up. He hooked the shaft under the offered jaw and heaved. Lifted erect, the buck went on over backward to sprawl on the ground. Fast as a cougar leaping to its kill, the Kid straddled the buck's body.

"The choice is yours," he growled in the Kaddo language, holding the lance ready to strike. "Do you live or die?"

Any lingering doubts as to the Kid's right to be called a Comanche died after his masterly display of lance handling. To the horse-Indians in general, and the Comanche most of all, the lance held a special position as a weapon. Only the bravest warrior carried one, accepting that he might be first into a fight and last out of it. Nor could he throw the lance, but must keep it in his hands and go close enough to use it.

Lying on the ground, the young buck suddenly realized just how precious life could be. He looked up, by the needle-sharp point and razor-edged blade of the lance to the savage face beyond and knew any hesitation would see the weapon thrust home. No man present would blame the Comanche—the Kid was all of that—for doing so under the circumstances.

"I live!" the buck croaked.

His companion came to a halt, standing dazed for

a moment. Then, letting out a snarl, he dived for the carbine. Through the exhaustion which filled him, Mark recognized the Kid. All wonder at how the Kid came to be on hand departed as Mark saw the danger to his friend. Shoving himself forward, Mark reached the Kid's side and curled his hand about the grips of the old Dragoon. Handling a strange weapon, from an awkward position, Mark could not produce his full blinding speed. Yet he drew fast enough. The buck's hands closed on the Spencer when the Dragoon boomed in Mark's hand. Dirt erupted into the Kaddo's face, temporarily blinding him. While Mark did not shoot for such an effect, it served his needs better than had the lead sunk into the buck. Spluttering, the brave dropped the carbine and sat knuckling his eyes in an attempt to clear them. When he finally managed to focus again, he found himself faced with the yawning muzzle of the Dragoon and lined blade of the lance. Again the Kid gave the choice and once more the recipient elected to live.

Holding the Colt, Mark expected the rest of the braves to jump him and the kid. None of the crowd moved but admiration flickered on more than one face. The Kaddo respected courage or dexterity in the use of weapons, both of which the two Texans had demonstrated.

"Are you all right, *amigo*?" asked the Kid.

"I'll do. Lifting the rock didn't trouble me, but shooting off this fool cannon like to bust my arm."

"Leather it, *pronto*. We can't fight our way through this bunch, so we'll have to talk our way out. Act like you expect your warrior's due."

"You're the Injun," Mark said dryly and dropped the Dragoon back into its holster. "Now let's see what happens."

"Get my brother a drink of water," the Kid said to Bear Killer. "He passed the test and is a free man."

"Do it," the chief ordered and a girl ran to obey.

"You say your name is Cuchilo. Are you the grandson of Long Walker?"

Once more the conversation went into Spanish. "I am," agreed the Kid.

A low mutter passed around the crowd for all knew the story of the treaty council at Fort Sherrard, especially the Kid's part in it.

"What brought you here, *Cuchilo*?" asked the old medicine man.

"I heard there were foolish words of war being spoken among the Kaddo and hoped to see you make lies of them."

Moon Watcher nodded, showing no surprise that the Kid had heard of the war talk. It had been the medicine man who told of the Kid's exploits at the treaty council, although Moon Watcher never went near the Fort.

"Why should we go the way of peace?" demanded Bear Killer.

"Because you will all be killed if you make war," the Kid replied.

"We have guns like the soldier-coats now," a young brave pointed out, waving his Winchester.

"Guns need bullets. You have few, the white men can get many. And they have wheel guns that can fire from where no rifle can reach them. They have guns which shoot bullets faster than a hundred men with rifles. The *Nemenuh* saw they could not fight such weapons. Do as my people did, ask the White Father in Austin to make a treaty with you. Go to him while you can still fight, not after you are beaten and must take whatever they offer."

"Already the white men come to take our land———" Bear Killer began, indicating the scared-looking Wycliffe who crouched on the ground with two lances lined on him.

"That's a lie," Mark interrupted and waved a hand toward the granite block. "That one lied to you. He planned to take the silver from this place and the men came to steal it from him.''

"And why did you come, big one?" Moon Watcher wanted to know.

"They killed a man who had been like a father to me. I followed them."

Every man present could understand Mark's motives and heartily approved of them. To hunt down the killer of a close friend ranked as a prime virtue and did nothing to lessen the esteem he gained by his actions. Moving forward, Moon Watcher looked at Mark with his head cocked on one side.

"Why did you listen to Hair Face's words in the tepee?"

"No man loses by listening to talk," Mark answered. "He told me much, but I did not say I would help him."

"That I know," Moon Watcher stated. "My son lay outside the tepee listening and he speaks your language."

A grin flickered across Mark's face, mirrored for a moment by the Kid. No matter that some Texans regarded Indian medicine men as fakes, both knew some to be remarkably shrewd, capable and with powers that no white man could fully understand. Certainly old Moon Watcher did not strike either as a charlatan and he seemed to have outfoxed Pegler.

"So you knew what he meant to do?" Mark said.

"I knew it well," agreed the old man. "And so did Bear Killer."

"That was why I let Hair Face have you," the chief went on. "So that Moon Watcher's son could listen as you talked."

"Do you want war, Bear Killer?" Mark asked bluntly.

"If the Great Spirit gave us medicine I would fight," the chief admitted.

"Was that why you put that one to the test?" Mark inquired nodding to where Wycliffe sat on the floor under guard.

"He came to our land to rob and killed Kaddo braves. One had a brother who called for revenge. I could not refuse."

"And what now, chief?" demanded the Kid. "Do you still lead the braves to war?"

"The medicine is broken, *Cuchilo*," Bear Killer replied. "We do not ride."

"Then meet the White Father in Austin. His heart is good to the Indian and he will treat you fairly."

"Will you and the big one speak for us if we do?" asked Moon Watcher.

"We will," agreed Mark. "We will arrange the day for you to come, but then we must ride. Our chief wants us with him as soon as possible."

"Don't he just," drawled the Kid in English. "Ole Devil'll be spitting eagle feathers and's like to have us on the blister end of a shovel for weeks if we don't get back to home real soon."

"Stay the night with us," suggested Bear Killer. "There is much to say."

"One thing I want, chief," Mark answered. "Him."

"He is yours, my brother," Bear Killer replied, following the direction of Mark's finger and eyeing Wycliffe in disgust. "Take him when you leave in the morning."

"Y—You saved my life, friend," Wycliffe said as Mark came toward him.

"Is Billy dead?" Mark growled.

"Not as I know of."

"Then, mister, you'd best hope I find him. If I don't, I'll see that *you* hang for Sailor Sam's murder in his place."

CHAPTER SIXTEEN

Not the Way to Use a Lance

STANDING behind a clump of bushes, with Rags's hand clamped over her mouth, Winnie wondered what had happened to make the men act in such a manner. She watched Billy Wycliffe and Augie moving cautiously down the slope, making use of every bit of cover available and carrying their rifles. Then a distant movement caught her eye and she looked in its direction.

Three men rode into sight through the trees and along the opposite side of the rolling ground before her. In the lead came a bare-headed Churn Wycliffe, seated on his fine bay mare, wearing an Indian buckskin shirt instead of his previous clothing. Slightly behind and to the right of Wycliffe rode a tall, slim youngster clad all in black and afork a magnificent white horse. At the left of Wycliffe, also just to the rear of the bearded man was—and Winnie could hardly believe her eyes—Mark Counter.

In some way, how she could not imagine, the blond giant had not only escaped from the Kaddo but met up with a friend and captured Churn Wycliffe. Even a naive country girl could figure that out. From the position they rode and the fact that they wore weapons while Wycliffe had none, it was obvious that the party did not travel as friends.

Then the meaning of Augie and Billy's actions

became clear to the girl. They planned to rescue
Wycliffe and probably kill the two men with him.
Unless she sadly misjudged Mark's nature, killing
him would be the only way to take away his prisoner.
In addition to her aversion to standing by and
watching murder done, she owed Mark her life. He
saved her from the Kaddo and she saw a chance to
repay him.

Feeling Winnie sag against him, Rags relaxed. Her
lack of opposition lulled him into a sense of false
security, so her next act came as a complete surprise.
Twisting her head, she managed to put her mouth
into position and sank her teeth around the base of
his thumb. At the same moment she hacked back at
his shin with her foot, a trick learned in childhood
scuffles, further weakening his hold. With a jerk she
tore free from his grasp and started to race down the
hill at an angle to take her behind the other two men
but toward Mark's party.

"Look out, Mark!" she screamed, shocked to see
how close he had come. "They're waiting for you!"

"You lousy bitch!" Rags howled, shaking his
hand then charging after her. "Just let me lay hands
on you."

The last part of his speech was all but drowned in
the crack of shots and a scream of a man in pain.
Snarling in fury, he plunged after the girl and ignored
what happened to his companions.

Mark and the Kid had been treated as honored
guests by the Kaddo. In addition to admiring his
strength, they respected what they thought to be
Mark's tolerance in merely throwing dust into the
young buck's face instead of driving the bullet into
him. After a good meal they had talked long on the
subject of making peace and had arranged for word
to reach the governor. At dawn Mark and the Kid
had collected Wycliffe, ready to return to Austin.

The Kaddo had even given Wycliffe's mare to the Texans so that he would not slow them down.

Clear of the canyon, the Kid had changed back into his normal clothing. While they allowed Wycliffe to ride with his hands free, he made no trouble. Watched over by two men highly skilled in the use of weapons, any attempt to escape would end in failure. As he rode along, Wycliffe had wondered where Billy might be. Knowing his nephew, heading for the safety of Austin had seemed the most likely place.

The Kid never relaxed when on the trail and kept constantly scouring the rolling wooded country through which they passed, eyes taking in every detail. In his growing years, he had excelled at the game of *Nanip'ka*, Guess Over The Hill, played to teach Comanche youngsters how to locate hidden enemies. That early training served him well. He had seen the partially concealed Rags and read significance in the man's withdrawal. While he doubted if either of his companions saw the watcher, the Kid decided to take precautions.

"Hold my lance, will you, Mark?" he said.

"Sure. What's up?"

"Nothing."

Which did not fool Mark for he had noticed that the Kid bent and slid out his rifle after handing over the lance. Wycliffe had heard the conversation and accepted it at face value. If he found the other two riding up closer to him, he thought little of it. Nor would looking back have told him anything, for the Kid held the Winchester hanging down out of sight on the far side of the horse.

Having ridden many dangerous trails with the Kid, Mark knew the signs. A slight jerk of the head directed Mark's attention toward the slope down which the two men made what they imagined to be an unobserved advance. Mark had recognised Billy

Wycliffe and tensed in his saddle. However he made no attempt to draw a weapon; to do so would warn the men that they had been discovered and might scare them off.

Up on the slope, Billy felt worried and uneasy when he saw that his victims moved at an angle which would carry them past his hiding place at a distance of some thirty yards or more instead of coming straight toward him. Augie had halted in a position about forty yards farther along the slope, kneeling behind a rock and lining his rifle. Sure the approaching men suspected nothing, Billy had cradled the butt of his Winchester against his shoulder and had aimed past his uncle at the broad chest of the blond giant.

Suddenly Winnie screamed out her warning. Finger on the trigger of his rifle, Billy stiffened at the sound. Then panic hit him. Already he knew how fast Mark could move and did not want to tangle with him in a gun fight. So he aimed and began to squeeze the trigger. Farther along the slope Augie had lined his rifle at the Kid, but twisted around with an angry growl on hearing the girl.

When the Kid heard Winnie, he knew the game was going to burst wide open at the seams. Jerking his left foot from the stirrup, he booted Wycliffe's bay hard in the ribs while starting to flip himself from the saddle. Taken by surprise, the mare leaped forward and carried her rider between Mark and Billy. Just an instant too late Billy saw the danger. Already the rifle's trigger had depressed far enough to free the hammer. The primer spat its flicker of flame into the bullet's powder charge, turning the black grains into a cloud of gas that hurled the bullet along the barrel. Lead meant for Mark ripped into Churn Wycliffe's body and tumbled him out of his saddle.

Landing cat-footed alongside his horse, the Kid darted forward. He threw up his rifle and fired in one fast move. Turning back to his work, Augie saw flame lick from the Kid's Winchester. Then something hot struck and seared across Augie's skull. His hat spun away and he staggered into the open before collapsing and lying perfectly still.

Mark also flung himself from his saddle but the lance he held prevented him from collecting the rifle from its boot. On landing he prepared to toss the primitive weapon away in favor of one of Colonel Colt's improved lifesavers. Then he saw Billy turn without making further attempts at fighting.

Cold rage welled up inside Mark, the deadly anger his great strength caused him to control most times. There fled the murderer of Sailor Sam, a coward without the guts to face an armed man. Gripping the lance between his two big hands, Mark hurled himself up the slope after Billy. The Kid also started running, levering another bullet home as he made for where Augie lay. There would be time enough to cut across and help Mark, should that prove necessary, after making sure the man could not take a further part in the affair.

Winnie fled down the slope with the speed of a cougar-spooked pronghorn. Behind her, pain from his bitten hand filling him with such rage that he forgot caution, Rags followed. Neither paid any attention to Billy as he went by them in the opposite direction. Nearer came the sound of Rags's running feet and Winnie stumbled around a large clump of bushes. A big shape loomed up in front of her and she swerved desperately without recognizing Mark for the moment.

Following the girl, Rags saw the blond giant before him and sent his hand grabbing for a gun. Like a flash Mark lunged, driving forward the lance. Steel sliced into Rags's belly, ripping it open. Picking up the screaming man on the lance's head, Mark flung him aside like a cowhand forking hay into the corral. Then, without a glance at either his victim or the girl, Mark took up the chase once more.

With the ambush chance ruined, both his enemies alive and his friends out of the game, Billy had the fear of death to spur him on. From the corner of his eye he saw the black dressed young man bounding up to cut him off. Behind him heavy feet thudded on the ground, drawing closer. Catching his foot on a root, he stumbled and, in trying to prevent himself from falling, dropped the rifle.

Reeling against the next tree, Billy flattened back to it and glared through wild eyes at the approaching blond giant. Snarling terrified curses, the young killer gripped his revolver's butt. The holster turned on its swivel and the Colt fired through the open bottom. While allowing a real fast first shot, such a holster made recocking its revolver difficult and did not lend itself to accuracy at any but close range. So the bullet missed, but Mark knew better than chance going any closer.

Back swung his right arm, carrying the lance over his shoulder, then hurling it forward. Its head struck Billy just under the center of the breast bone, penetrating with such force that it sank into the tree trunk behind and pinned him to it.

Slowly the red fighting rage ebbed from Mark and he stared at what he had done. Coming up, the Kid cradled his rifle across one arm and took in the scene with no great show of emotion.

"Damnit," he said indignantly, looking at Mark. "You're not supposed to *throw* a war lance."

"It seemed the best way to get rid of the fool thing," Mark replied. "How about his pard?"

"He's one lucky *hombre*. My bullet only creased his skull and he'll live to hang."

While Augie lived, he did not hang or even stand

trial. He had not been present when Sailor Sam was murdered and Winnie pleaded for him, saying that he had saved her from Billy. Guessing what would have happened to her had Billy been alone, Mark patched up Augie's skull, saw him safely back to Lake Travis and let him go free.

That came later.

Mark looked at the writhing body on the lance then growled to the Kid, "Go stop the gal coming here until I've got that lance out."

"Sure," the Kid replied. "We'll not tell her about the silver. The less who know about it the better."

Mark nodded grimly. The silver had cost Sailor Sam his life. Eleven of Churn Wycliffe's gang, Pegler and his hired help had all died through that ill-fated mine. As far as Mark was concerned, the silver could stay in the ground forever.